Was I halluci

Did tar fumes release some sort of preserved prehistoric mushrooms that were altering my reality? Because wherever I was – *whenever* I was – this was not my memory.

You have read enough, I think, to gather that I am too pragmatic to believe in the supernatural. And in truth, what was happening to me was not the stuff of ghosts and demons, of fairies and leprechauns. We are not talking about vampires here, like that largely debunked Aries VII report from a decade back.

No.

This was the metaphysical, some kind of reality just beyond the manicured fingertips of science.

This was not about bogymen. It was about a *boggyman.*

ATLAS ORIGINALS and the SEABOARD MONSTER GROUP

PROUDLY PRESENT

DIGGING DIRT:

SEEKING THE BOG BEAST

By Richard H. Levey

ATLAS ORIGINALS
Nemesis Group Inc
New York

Editor: Jeff Rovin
Publisher: Jason Goodman

This is a work of fiction. All characters, organizations, and events portrayed in this novel are either products of the author's imagination or are used fictitiously.

First Printing, July 2020

PROLOGUE

To human eyes, the world around it would have been undifferentiated darkness. But there were no human eyes. Not now. Not yet.

To its eyes, there was glorious nuance, the richness of the subterranean world. These were largely gradations of charcoal gray which shaded here and there to black. Some were the blackness of shadow; some were ants; most was the pitch of seeping, oozing, and occasionally dripping tar.

If humans were present, their eyes would have picked out spots of tawny root, the dull brown of an earthworm, the dead white of bone. Some of the bones were quite large and quite ancient, having fallen here, been picked clean here, been fossilized here ancient ages ago.

All of these flat tones were suffused by a gauzy haze. The mist was a combination of cool gaseous vapors from below: methane escaping from coal seams and hydrogen sulfide from the decomposition of sulfur compounds a greater distance underground.

It was an environment both natural and toxic to most life – life, that is, as it evolved on the surface of the earth.

This was not the surface of the earth.

The first humans to see this place, the tribe of the man Kromag, had called it *Awrr* – more a growl of revulsion and fear than a name. They had not penetrated far nor stayed long, having pushed through the clinging webs of great cave spiders, waded through substances adhesive and foul, ducked beneath low ceilings creeping with fetid moss, circled pits of flame so hot that their tiger-skin loincloths caught fire not from contact but from proximity. Yet they were grateful for those burning craters, for once they were beyond their light there was aught but that hopeless gray.

Over time, what those hardy Cro-Magnon had seen became a place of legend. From it sprang the myths of Orpheus and the forges of Vulcan and, later, belief in the kingdom of Satan.

And more recently, a cult that was the reason one had ventured from the bowels of the crust to stand, now – waiting.

It stood in a high-ceilinged cavern, with the world's most penetrating roots dangling from above. Had anyone been here to look they would not have seen it amid the flat, lifeless hues of the underworld. It,

7

too, was of such colors, and as unmoving as the stone on all four sides. Its eyes were open, sucking every particle of light from around it; golden, they were, and swirling – like a precious metal trapped in those pits seen by bold Kromag and his small party.

It waited for a human. One that would not possess the brawny courage of the primitive people but something no less compelling.

It had been below, far below, when it had sensed the male of the species. It had left its realm to follow a path that the earth itself remembered. It resounded with the footfalls, the familiar language – impossibly faint but only to those who were not listening.

The soil had carried the message.

The Bog Beast had a message too. A message it had not been able to deliver once before....

CHAPTER ONE

Call me a muckraker.

I have been called worse: my beat is Hollywood with a steaming serving of Washington swamp on the side. The two are intertwined, after all. Hollywood and DC are our two big industry towns. It was only natural they mate, like inbred members of royalty, and spawn the kind of warped, heartless, chemically preserved, surgically enhanced, mentally challenged, morally hollow people I write about.

The two communities need the press, yet neither is known for kindness or respect toward reporters – and vice versa. I get paid to interview and also to watch, from the shadows, the liaisons and drunken rants and drug buys that sell magazines and offer clickbait. I will dumpster dive, when necessary. There's a guy you'll be meeting soon, name of Arbogast. He's an ape-enforcer for Tinsel Town. I can't tell you how many times I've been threatened by guys like him. And not the "you'll never work in this town again" kind of hiss. More like the "you'll never walk again, kid," sort of growl.

They never followed through. Not with me, anyway. The reason was simple: I never had a story so hot, so dark, so deeply disturbing that it merited a threat or even a stiff-arm "back off."

Until now.

But I get ahead of myself and I cannot afford to do that. Not when I am about to do something so self-evidently stupid that I could die and die swiftly. So instead of moving on to my next assignment, like a sane and practical human being – investigating the Incinerating Vigilante who has been frying wrongdoers in New York – I am going to go back over it all, step by step, inch by inch, to make sure this makes some kind of sense.

My assignment was simple. Lynn Brandon, actress, dies of a reasonably common reason at a reasonably advanced age. Brandon had made enough notable films to be worthy of at least a dozen serious blog profiles, so she was penciled in for a mention in our September issue of *The Last Movie Magazine*.

I want to preface this by saying that I missed the days of writing for magazines like *Movie Monsters*. Low pay, pulp paper, no respect – sure, but at least the topics were fun, with a sense of wonder.

In the case of Lynn Brandon, I did my usual four-step "By Malcolm Leigh" obituary drill for celebrities.

Step one: check the basics of her personal life. Starter husband, second husband…then happy ending with her boy toy. Children: three with her second husband, who currently were as far from show business as they could get.

Step two: compile a list of directors and actors who worked with her and filter out the dead ones – no point chasing down someone who's underground.

Step three: watch her movies. Go back and edit list for step two, removing walk-ons, one-day-on-the-set cameos. I wanted people with dirt.

Step four: fill in the framework written based on steps one through three with quotes from anyone who answered emails, texts or – if they were local in Hollywood – knocks on the door. I got a few. Nothing brilliant, but they gave the profile legitimacy.

I sent the piece over to my editor, Jake Vincent, just before lunchtime on day four. I wanted to get out and clear my head, maybe grab a Not Dog. I hated writing about Hollywood stars. My job forced me to live in Granada Hills, in the famed and infamous Valley. It curdled my brain. That's probably why people liked my stuff. The contempt showed.

Vincent had my article for half an hour before calling.

"Good work," he said "if you were just starting out."

Uh oh. "What'd I miss?"

"Just a small detail. Nothing major. Nothing at all."

Which meant it was. I braced myself. Vincent was a pro at chasing dirt. His Manhattan office, the one the magazine rented from Lycosa Imports, was littered with movie star memorabilia from many decades. Most of it had been handed to him personally by stars, directors, writers, and producers. If he said something was missing, he was right – and it was going to be found before the article saw print.

Vincent continued. "You got that she was born Nicole Gordon, you say she acted under the name 'Nikie Gordon' until '74, but that's it."

"Isn't that it?" I asked. "She made some regional drive-in things that disappeared, took two years off, then re-emerged as Lynn Brandon."

"So you wrote."

Annoyed that I clearly was not getting out for lunch and a walk, I said, "You see those little curved lines surrounding that comment about why she got out of films in the '90s? That statement? Those are *quotes*. That was a quote from husband two, who I was lucky to get."

"He's an out-of-work actor. He'll talk to a wrong number. I'm surprised, after – what, fifteen years in the business that you missed it."

"Missed what?"

"I've got Romek Perkiel's set photos on my computer. Brandon was a brunette before her name change, but as soon as she got back from her two years off nobody ever saw her as anything but a blonde," he said. "She changed her name and her hair color, and right off the bat she started getting roles bigger than she'd ever had before."

I could picture Vincent leaning into his landline at his gunmetal desk in his tiny office. "That's where the damn story is. What happened, Mal?"

Those words changed my life.

CHAPTER TWO

An obituary that should have been a beefy photo caption had somehow evolved into a multi-page spread.

Lynn Brandon was at best a C-level actress in a string of B-level films. She had her fans – one of whom she hooked up with a decade after retiring in 1994 – and the barely leading lady even had a question in a popular trivia game. That's more than a lot of actresses get.

For Vincent, she had something else.

A secret.

Over a two-year period, Lynn had undergone the cosmetic changes that made her a fresh new face. At the time, few industryites would have asked why. Retreads were for plots. When it came to actresses, new was key.

So in 1974, Nicole "Nikie" Gordon vanished, and in the year of the American Bicentennial Lynn Brandon was presented to the world with full page ads in *Variety* and *The Hollywood Reporter* – the Cannes Film Festival issues, of course. Within the fan press, stories that would have focused on her lackluster past career were exchanged for access to new information. If the old stories about her were particularly lurid – and some were, especially from her days as a cocktail waitress – cash was added to the publishers' pockets.

Thus, a star was reborn.

But in 2020, what was *new* about Lynn Brandon was her secret. Nobody had ever gotten the story about her time off or her transformation. Sure, sure – career do-over. But for twenty-three months and change? In the life of a young actress, that was prime real estate. More than anything else, that period was what turned Vincent on about her.

Plus this. After retiring, Lynn had lived an unlisted life. For two decades, access to her was limited to a post office box. The day after Vincent bounced my obituary back to me, I wasted my time trying to talk with her kids. Two had been estranged from her for years and did not want to be found. The third refused to comment. Grief, he claimed. I would have asked to quote him if I hadn't heard a Jacksonville Jaguars game in the background. Still, I threw long as the call ran out:

"One word to describe her off-camera?"

"Here's two," he said before punching out. "A. Mess."

A good line, but not without context. Was she a personal mess? A professional mess? Was there a third species of mess?

Fortunately – because I did not like disappointing Vincent and he didn't like me *to* disappoint him – the president of Lynn Brandon's fan club responded to my email on the morning of day two and I was soon in touch with Lynn's boy toy, the one she'd been keeping company with for the latter part of her life. Of course, it helped that the beau and the enthusiast were the same man.

So her last paramour, Milton Whitestone, was my first substantial contact for the elusive new angle. He had run her fan club and website before they had met, and had kept them going for years after she had retired. Maybe it was that level of dedication that had caused Lynn to shack up with the guy. Or maybe it was because when he wasn't carefully slipping signed, 8 x 10 glossies into manila envelopes, he'd proven himself a pretty fair accountant. Supposedly his fees matched her residuals, according to a lawsuit filed by the one kid I'd managed to track down. The claim was settled out of court.

I drove out to see Whitestone, who did not ask me about my trip to their – now his – Pasadena bungalow. He *was* grief-stricken. And distracted.

Whitestone apologized for not getting back to me sooner – there were details and duties regarding Lynn's estate. There was also regret: she would have appreciated the last bit of media attention, he told me. She had been cremated, and there would be a

21

ceremony by the Pacific for scattering the ashes at some point.

I glanced at his desk. At his laptop. At the open inbox that did not seem to have a lot of anything stacked on top of my email. Milton Whitestone may have convinced his late paramour that legions of fans still wanted information about her, but it sure seemed as though that information was flowing one way. Maybe that was the reason he was so eager to share with a reporter who actually showed up on his doorstep.

Whitestone straightened some mementoes, grabbed a shoebox, and then we moved from the living room to the kitchen. Over barely drinkable instant coffee we had a conversation about her films, most of which I hadn't known before I'd looked her up. But I was able to recite titles, and he happily picked up on each and told second- and thirdhand stories about them.

"Can you imagine what it is like to live with the most beautiful woman in the world?" Whitestone asked me.

I couldn't, partly because the world's most beautiful women were rarely in the dating market for mid-level reporters. Nor did I dispute his description of her. She was beautiful – beautiful enough, anyway.

"I was in my mid-30s when I first met her – of course, I had been a fan for years before that," he told me. "She never played a part, no matter how it was written, one dimensionally. Every role had something extra."

"Cagney called it 'a little bit of business,'" I added helpfully, trying to bond with the guy.

He continued as if I hadn't spoken.

"Lynn gave it all a little sadness, a little mystery, a little humor, sometimes all three at once. I was blown away by her."

Whitestone picked up the shoebox, pulled out a shoe, and handed it to me. "What do you think?"

His eyes were fixed on it, so I handled the beige pump as though it were the Holy Grail. I held the thing to my eye, trying to look as though I knew anything about women's shoes.

"She was tall," I said. "She wouldn't have needed much of a heel."

Whitestone grinned. "This is one of her secrets!"

"How many secrets did she have?" I asked leadingly.

He didn't bite. "There's a lift built into it. Her left leg was a little shorter than her right. Her shoes were custom made, so she could walk straight."

"Did she have an accident?" I asked, half-hoping she had; it would be something to write about.

"No, she was born that way," Whitestone shrugged. "Nobody knew it. She was an exercise fanatic. Kept herself fit. Was able to play all her parts without limping, unless her character was hurt." He grinned again. "Then, she was a natural."

I filed the fact, but just barely. There was no way I could present it to Vincent as The Secret Lynn Brandon Kept from Her Fans. I would get the missing two years or I would incur his wrath.

"What are you going to do with her shoes?" I asked, returning the treasure.

"I'm not sure," he said. "I offered them, along with the boxes of her papers, to a library at UCLA. I thought they could catalog them. But they wanted me to pay them for taking them. Imagine!"

I was imagining. I was imagining several boxes of Lynn Brandon memorabilia quietly moldering somewhere, forgotten until maybe a grandkid came looking for them.

"Where are her papers now?" I asked.

"In the attic. I haven't cataloged them myself, yet."

Enduring Whitestone's ramblings earned me the privilege of climbing two flights of stairs and sneezing my way through boxes of *Fangoria* magazine, newspaper clippings, and a series of photographs. Many were meticulously identified with the names, dates, and locations of what they captured, while on some Lynn had scrawled personal comments about the quality of a script, the fee she was offered – handy professional information.

Nestled among these treasures were two boxes of the life Lynn Brandon had as aspiring actress Nicole Gordon. One was labeled 1969-1972, and the other 1973-1974. These boxes had been heavily sealed with tape, which I took the liberty of slicing open. What the hell, I was in that stuffy attic with Whitestone's permission, and based on the dust surrounding the boxes it was clear nobody had looked at them during the last few decades. If later challenged, I would apologize. It is far easier to obtain forgiveness than permission.

The first box was stuffed with headshots for Nicole Gordon – "Nikie," as they were labeled. It also held receipts for acting classes, a few pieces of clothing in plastic bags with dates, but not names, on them, and a couple of scripts. It contained a mug and an ashtray from one of the major studios. Plates from studio commissaries. Keepsakes of someone new to the business.

The second carton lacked the poignancy of such sentimental items. It held a standard contract from Worldly Pictures, Gordon's first studio. The actress had circled the paltry salary, drawn a line to producer Irv Schloss's name and amended the contract with the words "Still sucking!"

There were more film scripts, neatly stacked in the order in which she'd worked on them. The Internet Movie Database had a slightly different order, probably due to it relying on release dates as opposed to shooting dates.

But one script, *Tomb of Frankenstein*, had never been made. IMDb listed it as "postponed" as of 1974, and apparently it had never been restarted. A shame, for Nikie Gordon: the highlighted sections and written pencil notes indicated it would have been her breakout role, two years before she actually had one.

There were two folded sheets of paper tucked between pages in the script. These turned out to be a cast and crew list, on which someone – probably Nikie, based on the handwriting – had noted descriptions of each person. Evidence of a new kid on the set, looking to ingratiate herself.

There was also a legal agreement "Nicole Gordon" signed in late 1974, which gave her a substantial cash bonus and promised her prime roles in three movies. It discussed media access and privacy guarantees. It seemed pretty one-sided – in favor of the actress, which was as strange then as it is now.

Surprisingly, there was no time frame assigned to those roles, which was a good thing: she wouldn't finish filming the third of them until 1978.

Nikie's handwritten signature at the bottom of this document was shakier than the one in the script, but it was definitely hers, although with larger, loopier letters, as though she had been wearing a mitten.

I am not necessarily proud of what I did with some of these items. Not proud as a human being, I mean. As a reporter, what I did was first rate. I stuffed the script, the legal agreement, which had proof of her penmanship, and some of the photos into my shoulder bag, intending to turn them over to

Vincent as "previously unseen treasures from the unknown life of Lynn Brandon." Photographs of a few dozen pages of text were easily captured by my phone.

The boxes from Nikie's later life – now being lived as Lynn Brandon – didn't offer any insight into her identity change, or anything else. I added two headlights photos picked from a file of half-dozen fetish shots –UGH BURN THESE! was written on the outer envelope – to my swag stash. It wasn't anything incriminating – think Bettie Page light – but I hadn't seen them before. If Vincent hadn't either, Lynn Brandon was going to get a whole section in the September issue.

About an hour into my digging, Lynn's domestic partner – which is what he was, I later learned – interrupted me with an offer of iced tea and a tuna fish sandwich at the kitchen table. I suspected he was having concerns about what I *might* be doing up here, which was, in fact, exactly what I *was* doing. I turned down the sandwich. Even if the instant coffee wasn't proof enough of his culinary skills, it's not my thing.

"Finding everything you need?" Whitestone asked.

I didn't want him to be so excited by anything I said that he would go bounding up to the attic and see the unsealed boxes. At the same time, I wanted to give him a crumb.

"You've got some great stuff, but I am missing a few things. What did she say about making *Tomb of Frankenstein*?"

Whitestone looked puzzled. "That isn't one of hers," he said.

"I think it might have started production in 1974. I don't think it was finished."

"Oh, her old life," he said dismissively. "We didn't discuss that time very much. She regarded her career as having begun in 1976." He snickered. "She used to kid about missing out on the bicentennial Best New Starlet awards."

As open as Whitestone had been about Lynn's post-1976 career, he was equally closed about her earlier years. He parried questions about her home life growing up, her high school friends, her childhood. She hadn't discussed her previous persona, so he wouldn't either. For all intents, Nicole Gordon had been left on the set of *Tomb of Frankenstein*. If I wanted to know what had happened, I would have to look elsewhere.

To that end, my next stop would be the Worldly Pictures lot – at least, what used to be the lot in 1974. Thanks to Vincent – who called an old source who used to drive a limousine in Hollywood – it turned out that the person who was going to help me travel time was producer Irv Schloss.

CHAPTER THREE

Irv Schloss was not at the studio lot anymore.

Irv Schloss lived in a warehouse for human beings.

It wasn't listed that way, of course. Stokesay Heights was an apartment complex for hundreds of residents aged 65 and up. It was on reasonably well-kept grounds near a golf course. There wasn't a high school, playground, or water park within ten miles. I was more than thirty years too young to live there, and when my time comes I can only hope death finds me before a Stokesay Heights sales agent does.

Schloss welcomed me like a cousin – one he might've liked, one who had never asked him for a job or loan. He was waiting in the vestibule, seated on a sunny window seat with a view of a young woman visiting her grandmother.

Smoking wasn't allowed but his breath still smelled of cigar, probably left over from when he was a mogul. He welcomed me warmly and showed me to a patio off his first-floor lodgings. The terrace overlooked a pond with a fountain that misted the air pleasantly.

We sat in comfortable wicker chairs, although every few minutes he would painfully stand up and go inside his apartment to retrieve one artifact or another – a lobby card, a prop, a photograph – to help illustrate his narratives.

Most of his stories starred Irv Schloss as the hero or the romantic lead, if how he interacted with his actresses and starlets could be called romance. How he found this star. How he bedded that starlet, told to me in conspiratorial whispers. And then there was the topic that got him most excited: how he took stories from obscure 1950s pulp magazines and secondhand twenty-five cent paperbacks and turned them into moneymakers.

"My secret was marketing and monsters," he said. "For twenty years, my approach at Worldly was to use cheap sets and cheap talent, come up with a good tag line or a good gimmick, and spend on the monsters." He leaned forward in his chair, gripping the armrests, fixing me with watery gray eyes. "Don't... skimp... on the monsters!" He sat back and laughed. "That's how I said it to my board, when they complained about what I spent on the costumes for *The Beast with Forty Faces* and *Tendrils from the Moon*."

Schloss started on what sounded like a well-honed sales pitch. His eyes focused on nothing, and I got the sense he was no longer talking to me, but to a bunch of long-ago studio execs who had been crying poverty.

When he was finished, Schloss stood and crooked a finger at me.

"Lemme show you something."

He went into his apartment and moved toward a side room. The shades were drawn and the room smelled like Lynn Brandon's attic. I caught up with him as he was walking toward a polished wooden base adorned with a ferocious Tyrannosaur-like head on one side. Mounted next to it was a claw holding a bitten-in-half subway car. The whole thing was the size of an end table.

Affixed to the front was a brass plaque with the inscription "Irv – next time, YOU get lunch! Love you, cheapskate! – Elias Harrysen."

I just stared.

"The best!" Schloss said.

He did not need to. My first professional article was about Harrysen for *Movie Monsters*. I received a public scourging, but also an essential cult following, by proclaiming his film *Earth vs. the Venusian* was superior to *Citizen Kane*.

Harrysen's name was a gold standard in special effects craftsmanship. For decades during the mid-20th century, directors who wanted to scare the pants off America went to his studio. When Harrysen destroyed cities through earthquakes, fire, and flood, moviegoers called their mothers after leaving the theater, "just making sure you're okay."

His monsters? They breathed, glared, snarled, and lived. People wept when they died. Well, kids did anyway.

My eyes rose from the plaque to the creation above. I gawked.

"That's from *Cragakin Released*!" I said. "He ripped his way through New York City. When I was a kid I wanted to visit and see if they had rebuilt the elevated trains and the Empire State Building."

Schloss laughed. "You liked Cragakin? He was the reason New York put more subway lines underground. Prove me wrong."

"I didn't see *Cragakin Released* when it first came out," I said. "I watched it on TV as a kid, and it was the first time I'd ever seen a monster tearing through an American city. Until Cragakin, I thought monsters only attacked Japan."

40

"Television?" Schloss spat. "You missed half of it! It needed big screen size, scope!"

"I know," I said. Normally I want my interview subjects to do the talking, but I gushed my love for Cragakin. "I couldn't believe how good it looked when I finally got a high-def Blu-ray," I told Schloss. Now I knew why. The puppet head and claw Schloss showed me must have been used for close-up work. The detail was incredible.

"Harrysen was a genius," Schloss said quietly. "He was a genius when I started working with him in '62 on *Liftoff to Luna*, and he was a genius until the end."

We went back to his terrace. Schloss now seemed tired and heavy-limbed. But while his voice was quiet, it was also strong.

"I became a movie producer because I can't tell stories," he started. "Not like a writer or a Harrysen can. But now I want to tell you a story. I haven't talked about this for 45 years, and anyway I never had anyone I could talk to about it. But I'm tired of carrying it. Maybe now I get some absolution.

"So, Mr. Leigh, let me tell you about *Tomb of Frankenstein*. And maybe you won't judge me too harshly."

I was ninety percent reporter and, suddenly, ten percent fanboy as I tapped on my iPhone recorder. The unfinished film had a history. I would be the one to find out what it was.

"In 1974, after more than a decade of not skimping on monsters, just before shooting started, I fired the best special effects man in the world from my movie," Schloss started. "There were a lot of reasons. See, we had been making biker movies since the late sixties – *Vroom Devils*, *Helmet Honeys*, *Vroom Devils Meet Helmet Honeys*. Then suddenly that whole thing was out of gas and we decided to go back to monsters. We had a saying: 'When in doubt, go BOO!' Even before we shot a foot of film, Worldly Studios planned a big marketing campaign planned for *Tomb of Frankenstein*. They were going to sell it hard as the studio's first picture with computer-aided effects. Those graphics were kind of cartoony but they were new. The lightning and explosions would be cheaper than Harrysen's hand-crafted work and if we covered them with smoke and mist – well, who'd notice?"

"You're saying that Harrysen was obsolete?"

"Like the dinosaurs he created in *World of Things*. But more than that, he was expensive. Worldly needed that money to spend on ads. We had another saying: 'When in doubt, SELL HARD!' That meant Harrysen had to go. Reluctantly, I backed the decision.

"Marketing and monsters," he said, sighing. "People always came second at Worldly, unless they generated box office."

"Like Lynn...I mean, Nicole Gordon?"

"Like Nikie. I'll get to her."

Schloss may have been "reluctant" in 1974 but the slumping man before me seemed openly repentant. Whether he felt like talking, needed to confess, or both, he held nothing back.

But...I'll let him tell it in his own words:

"Ah, those days..." he began.

CHAPTER FOUR

The days before *Tomb of Frankenstein* and computers. The big, flat, endless open roads of California and Nevada were our backlot. They offered most of the sets these pictures needed. For interior scenes, we had one bar that we changed a little from picture to picture. It had been a malt shop in our 1950s pictures, the *Hot Grease* hot rod series.

Crews loved that set. Why not? For the biker pictures it was a functioning bar.

It was back to being a soda shop for *Tomb of Frankenstein*, though we kept a supply of booze for the crew to use after hours. That was where I found Harrysen the day he was let go. His old buddy, hair stylist John Pierce, was just leaving. Pierce scowled at me like I'd just dented his Corvette. I didn't blame him.

Harrysen was at the bar and his slouch indicated he had been there a while.

I approached him, scuffing my feet so as not to startle the special effects wizard. He still didn't seem to hear me. I rested a hand on his shoulder.

"Elias–"

"I don't want to hear it, Irv."

"Please, it's not you."

He rolled a shoulder to throw off my hand. "Go away."

"Not until you've heard me out. You know that Worldly has always been big on gimmicks – "

"'*Know*'? Who came up with the Sketch-o-Rama Draw the Monster Pads?"

"You did – "

"Whose idea were 1-D movies, Irv? Who came up with that, right at this bar?" Still staring at the bar, he thumped his chest with a fist.

"You did, Elias. Which is why you should understand better than anyone that computers in film production are the same. A trick. A fad. Only much more expensive. Monstrously expensive, a *Cragakin*-size budget buster, which is why we have to make cuts."

"Double the cost and half as good, Irv. You know it. I know it. The penny-squeezers at the studio know it. For 25 years they've been coming to me to do all the impossible special effects nobody else would try. Me! On my own! I don't have a bunch of...of crew cut screwdriver kids and hippie cartoonists working for me."

"Elias, you are the best, we know that –"

"And they don't care. Everything I did. I made dog skeletons fight cat skeletons! I created Jetor, a 747 possessed by an alien ghost!"

"His fight with Boathemoth is an acknowledged classic."

"Acknowledged by who? By Worldly, which made a fortune off me?"

It didn't seem possible, but the now-unemployed man managed to slump further.

"Elias, let me take you home –"

"I'm going to my studio. I have some calls I got to make. I want to talk to my union rep."

"Elias, what good is that going to do you? The president of the union has been friends with the head of Worldly since their Army days. Look, this will pass. They will come to you, you'll see.

Meantime, we'll talk to some of the theme parks. You've done beautiful work for us. We'll find other work for you."

"Sure. I always wanted to design a Ferris wheel that eats its riders."

"Y'know, that's not a bad idea."

"Screw you, Irv. My movies are dead. Dead as the big screens that have shrunk to tiny screens. Soon they'll be even smaller. You guys…you killed the joy."

"Elias, let me get you out of here. I've got the convertible. Let's take a drive into the hills. Santa Barbara. We'll get some clean air. You like the Painted Caves up there – "

Harrysen held his glass in front of his face and looked at his reflection. It was broken, distorted. He swirled the dark contents of the glass, causing the liquor to slosh high against the sides. He grinned at his sinister face, which shifted as the scotch moved round. I was willing to bet, right then, that he was thinking of some new monster. That was Harrysen. He never stopped working, thinking, creating. I felt even more crappy and guilty then.

The special effects man slammed the glass down, slid from his barstool, and stood unsteadily. "I'm not going to Santa Barbara and I'm not going home. I wanna ride the tour trolley while my ID is still good."

"Want company? You did such a hell of a job with that…that's one of the biggest attractions in –"

"Irv, just let me be. I'm gonna do that, then I'll go to my office to pack. Make some phone calls on Worldly's dime."

"Sure. Sure."

Harrysen staggered out into the late afternoon and I let him be. I was embarrassed and I clearly was not doing him any good. I didn't find out till later, 'til I pieced things together, what happened next.

Harrysen caught up with one of the studio's trams as it was leaving the terminal. The car was three-quarters full, and he slipped to the back so he could savor tourist reactions. The ride itself held no surprises for him – he had designed it, down to the animatronic claw which seemingly plucked the trolley from its tracks before depositing it at the ride's end. The tour guide told me that she saw him close his eyes so he could enjoy the gasps of tourists without distraction. She saw him smile.

They rode through the four seasons, which showed how movie magicians like him created snow and desert heat and everything in between. Sold a lot of Worldly sweatshirts after that winter excursion.

From there it was a journey through ravaging nature. Lightning storms cracked all around the tourists, who jumped and screamed. I'm told Harrysen laughed at that. Tidal waves always just missed the trolley. A tornado spun and howled and flung debris at riders – behind safety glass, of course.

Next the trolley rumbled through the ravaged cities of the world. Cities Harrysen had destroyed in his films. Stomped Tokyo. Clawed, bitten, and tumbled New York. Shattered Los Angeles. London, Paris, Washington DC, each with its iconic structures toppled, smashed, incinerated by dinosaurs, dragons, demons, or extraterrestrials. Harrysen had wanted to include a ruined Rome from *Twenty Thousand Miles to Hell.*

"What about a lava pit?" he had asked but the studio heads had nixed the idea as too dangerous. Pity. He could almost smell the sulfur.

When Harrysen did open his eyes, he did not see the exterior wonders he had created but the incredible mechanisms behind them. There were no apparent steam pipes, sprinkler heads, or gas jets. Everything had been perfectly camouflaged. The perfect crime in set design, he told himself.

At Trolley Station 33, Harrysen bailed. Station 33 was right where a giant ape, or at least the giant roaring head and arm of an ape, menaced the trolley. A perfect distraction. Even better, for

Harrysen, it was close to the master control room for the ride and several soundstages.

Harrysen shot the trolley guide a quick thumbs up and went over the side just as the car slowly rounded a curve. Alone now, he ducked behind a building façade and slipped through an unmarked exit – also carefully camouflaged. And then he was in a control room.

Anyone who ever wanted to feel like God would have gotten their wish in one of Elias Harrysen's control rooms. Closed-circuit cameras monitored and controlled every part of the tour – alien planet surfaces, post-apocalyptic wastelands, frontier towns, and Gothic castle interiors. Several monitors displayed the *Tomb of Frankenstein* soundstage, where lights could flicker, staircases could collapse, and an entire building could go up in flames at the whim of whoever was in the control seat.

That whoever currently was a somewhat drunk, and very angry, Elias Harrysen.

Over on the set of *Tomb of Frankenstein*, Andrei Iovan was stumbling around. He was intentionally stumbling. It was his way of getting into character – Frankenstein's Monster, a role he had played in a half-dozen movies back in the day. He was a broad-shouldered circus strongman before he turned to acting, and his shoe lifts brought his height to a towering six-foot-eight. He pulled with annoyance at the coat the costumer had given him.

There were two truths about Andrei Iovan. Nobody could play the monster like him, the man who had originated the role decades earlier, and Iovan couldn't play much else. Out of makeup, he was just a bad actor. In makeup, he was a bad person who *thought* he was a great actor. Today, he was in full makeup.

Iovan paused in the middle of the rehearsal.

"Why am I wearing a lab coat?" he loudly asked the air, assuming somebody would answer. Someone always did.

Director John Davies stepped from the shadows. Assistant Director Tessa Whiting was at his elbow.

"Because you're a mad scientist," Davies answered, bracing for a fight.

"The monster is not a scientist," Iovan said. "The monster is always a monster. *'Raarrgh,'* and like that. Nobody is going to believe the monster is a scientist. Why not make him an airplane pilot while you're at it?"

"Andrei, please," Davies finally looked up from his script, where he had been penciling last-minute ideas. "The monster is a scientist because it is central to the plot. Strange goings-on in the Frankenstein Monster's lab."

"Yeah, brain transplant, I read the script – "

"Right. This Frankenstein's monster is smart," Davies said.

"The brain of a schoolteacher isn't enough. Can we say he took some night classes?" Iovan asked. "Maybe in the University of Ingolstadt's Continuing Ed division?"

"Sure. Sure, you play it that way."

"Okay, that works."

"Good. So now he's like Einstein with bolts on his neck. *That's* why he needs to wear the lab coat."

Iovan extended his arms and twisted like a helicopter rotor. "It's not even cut right," he grumbled.

"It isn't his, remember? It belongs to Dr. Frankenstein, who was half his size even before you squeezed him into a wall safe."

"But I can't move, see?" Iovan complained. "Look, it's the *Tomb of Frankenstein*. Tomb. I have a mortician's coat that fits perfectly for that. Let me put that on."

Iovan was wasting time, time cost big bucks, even on a rehearsal day, and Davies had had enough.

"Linda?" he called for the wardrobe girl. "Adjust Mr. Iovan's lab coat, please."

"Right away, Mr. D."

"Thanks. Now Andrei? Don't be a prat. Please focus on getting the feel for your shoes. When the sparks – techies – arrive, I'm going to need light-meter readings of you and Nikie."

Iovan unhappily stomped away, floorboards creaking under him.

"Careful," Davies called to him. "That floor is supposed to break away later."

Davies turned to Tessa and whispered. "No sense in that S.O.B. falling through it when the cameras aren't rolling."

It was then Nicole "Nikie" Gordon bustled onto the set, trailing clouds of gorgeous.

"Everything all right?" she asked the director.

"Everything is perfect," Davies told the top of her dirndl, which was laced up tightly under her breasts. "Please tell me you don't need me to explain why your character would be wearing high heels in a laboratory."

"My character will be wearing high heels in a laboratory because that's who my character is, and it's my job to make it work," Nikie said sweetly.

Davies relaxed. The girl had a big part and Davies hadn't worked with her before. But she seemed to be compliant.

"How are you doing?" he asked.

"Oh, fine," Nikie said. "Is there anything I can do for *you*?"

Davies wasn't used to actors being solicitous of him. Soliciting him, yes, but not making a genuine attempt to be pleasant.

"I am fine, thank you," he said. "Get comfortable with the set. For the next twenty-one days it's going to be your home. You should move around like it is." Davies gestured broadly. "But don't disturb the cobwebs. Audiences expect mad scientist homes to be webby."

"I guess feather dusters aren't standard equipment in the laboratory," she quipped.

"Stop breaking my concentration," Iovan complained to both of them.

Silence fell on the doomed set – doomed in the film, doomed in reality – and Nikie became reflective, introspective as she got into character. John Pierce later told me she had been wired that morning. Her first-day excitement had found her at the studio early, and she had explored every part of the big sets – not just the lab but the grand foyer of the Castle of Frankenstein, marveling at the French doors that lead to a grassy hillside, resisting the urge to wrap herself in the heavy velvet draperies, but giving in to climbing up a staircase which, through movie magic, would eventually appear to lead to her bedroom, even if it currently ended at a painted door.

Davies turned back to Tessa.

"I'm going to get some of these notes typed," Davies said. "When I get back, we'll do the run through. I want the extras on-set – let's say four o'clock?"

"They will be here, torches aglow," the young woman replied.

Nikie noticed that director's exit came quickly, as Iovan was clomping his way back to the mainstage. Even through the grotesque, yellowish monster makeup she could see the actor was displeased about something.

One of Iovan's big thumbs jerked over his shoulder as he approached Tessa.

"What's *that* thing?" Iovan asked, pointing to the edge of the set.

If Elias Harrysen were not distracted by his inner rage, he might have seen something in the shadows of the *Tomb of Frankenstein* set as it appeared on his closed-circuit monitors. There were always things in the shadows of an Elias Harrysen monster mansion set, because he had put them there. This one, he hadn't.

Harrysen was focusing on a control bank. The studios had access to water reserves not available to the average California homeowner. Harrysen had tamed these resources through an elaborate series of large pipes and custom fittings to create the floods and storms on the tour.

Now was the time to showcase them.

In his angry and inebriated state, Harrysen had conceived a swan song for *Tomb of Frankenstein* that studio executives – and the industry – would never forget. Maybe that was what he had seen in his glass at the bar: waves swishing this way and that. I don't know. What I *do* know is that the plan he had evolved was as epic as anything he had ever done.

He was going to flood the world. Or at least the set of *Tomb of Frankenstein*.

That "thing" Iovan had pointed at was standing immobile near a dusty dark red curtain. It

64

was easily seven feet tall. It loomed over Iovan: bipedal, skeletal, and thickly covered with black viscous tar to which clung a variety of rooty vegetation. Its frame was vaguely human, with accentuated shoulders, hipbones, and an outsized cranium. Its large almond-shaped eyes were a dull yellow and it had the stench of compost about it.

Nikie gave a yip of fright. "Where did *that* come from? What a scary thing! He looks so real!"

"Is this some trick of Davies's?" Iovan demanded. "Some *ploy*?"

"It isn't in the script," Tessa remarked and jumped on her walkie-talkie.

Iovan was not happy. The script called for only one monster, and he was it. Two monsters would mean half the attention.

"Hey, you! Mud-man!" Iovan said, lumbering toward the spindly newcomer.

"He smells," Nikie said, pinching her nose shut against its sulfur reek and half-turning.

"This whole thing stinks!" Iovan said. "Where are you from, jerk?"

Davies was already crashing through the studio door, having been alerted by the assistant director.

"I can tell you where it's going," the director howled. "Elias Harrysen's workshop. It's probably one of his old jobs. Must be his going-away present to us."

Apparently emboldened with relief that his role as main horror attraction wasn't going to be upstaged, Iovan moved toward the newcomer.

"C'mon fella!" the actor taunted as he reached for the protruding chin of the stoic figure. "Let's see who's behind that mask!"

Iovan pulled. Nothing happened – but only for a moment. The yellow eyes narrowed, the color ripened to gold, and the thing exuded a strong odor that was part fertilizer, part stink bug.

"Hold on!" Davies said suddenly. "This is no joke. It's for real!"

That only made Iovan tug harder. Suddenly, the creature drew its elbows toward the center of its body and its hands opened, reaching for Iovan. Tessa later said that the joints sounded like twigs snapping.

It grabbed Iovan under the armpits and hoisted him as if he were on overhead wires. No one moved; the action was too shocking, too sudden.

And then the Frankenstein Monster was airborne. Big Andrei Iovan described a flailing arc nine or ten feet above the floor as the thing effortlessly hurled him into the staircase bannister. There was a splintering, crunching sound. The bannister remained intact. Iovan's spine did not.

Suddenly, it started to rain on the set.

Davies was the first to react.

"Someone call security!" the director shouted. "Tell 'em we got a madman loose on Studio 33!"

Nikie was the second to react. "Oh Lord! My hair will be ruined!"

Davies later recalled that it seemed a small, unimportant thing to say – but no one knew what was happening, or why, as one surprise replaced another.

Tessa was the third to react, shouting, "Hey! Who turned on the rain machine? It's not in the script!"

Sparks began to shoot from the live electric cables.

"Evacuate the soundstage!" Davies shouted as he ran to check Iovan. The actor, now dead weight, had been correct: it would have been more appropriate if he had worn the mortician's coat.

The rain intensified. Valves opened in the wall baseboards and water rushed out. Electric systems shorted with loud pops, plunging the soundstage into semi-darkness and adding to the chaos.

Water was geysering from several locations, including the hilly area that lay just beyond the foyer set. The water overwhelmed the drainage system and was pooling on the house set. Nikie, soaked and scared, was finally moved to action. She bolted across the foyer floor.

Which, as the *Tomb of Frankenstein* script required, collapsed under the combined stresses of water, impact, and day laborer construction quality. With a crash, water, floor beams, and Nicole Gordon disappeared into a deeper-than-needed pit below the soundstage.

Davies had Tessa organize the crewmembers while he headed toward my office.

CHAPTER FIVE

Schloss interrupted his narrative to go to the bathroom.

I sat alone and considered what he had told me. I was here to write about Lynn Brandon, or Nicole Gordon. But now she had a co-star.

A creature.

A thing that was not, apparently, of Elias Harrysen's making.

A beast of some kind that reeked like a bog. Something about all this suggested the name. I put it in my notes: Bog Beast. And then I waited for Irv Schloss to return.

As I sat there, I had the strangest sense that I knew more than I had been told. Or rather I *intuited* more than I had been told. I had seen the photos from the set, the lighting tests. The pictures of Nikie. But now I felt as if I were there, somehow seeing them through different eyes.

Yellow-golden eyes.

CHAPTER SIX

The Bog Beast was confused.

Normally it would draw strength and stability from the nitrogen in the earth. But it was getting no nitrogen pull from the hills of the outdoors set. It was also aware of the hum of active electricity – a hum that had been throughout the set when all the lights had been on, but which had become localized since the lights went off and the water started.

The fate of the girl-human was the more pressing concern. Aside from a single moan, the creature hadn't heard anything from her. Judging from how she had reacted to relatively little amounts of moisture earlier, she was now completely out of her element.

These humans show little concern for each other, the creature thought. *One has left, and I sense no others are coming.*

The creature moved to the hole, jumped down past ruined floorboards and machinery, and found Nikie bobbing in the pit of rapidly rising water. Furnishings carried by the rushing liquid were splashing down around, and sometimes on top of, her. The water surrounding her was muddy with a red tinge.

High ground for her first. Then, I have questions. The creature grabbed Nikie by her hair and arm. It felt a cracking in her shoulder. It heard a soft cry of pain. *She is fragile. Are they all this fragile?*

The creature shifted its grasp of Nikie, lifting her out of the hole and placing her on a toppled bookshelf near its lip. It hoisted itself out of the hole and moved the young actress again, this time to the staircase, which was mostly above water. The body of Andrei Iovan still hung over the bannister like a wet rag.

The humans did not menace me, the creature thought. *Only this beast. It attacked without cause. Perhaps it was some manner of mutant. An artificial creation of these humans. It could not be allowed to continue without acknowledging that all have a right to live.*

The creature brushed Iovan off the bannister so Nikie would not be crowded when she came to. The actor's body landed with an ugly splash and began to float toward the hole: the collapsed floor would not be denied its monster.

The creature did not notice. Its thoughts were elsewhere. It knew nature – was part of nature – and had elemental understanding of earth and water.

This is not the way nature acts, it thought. *And the dirt and hills are wrong. I do not sense their gentleness, their age, their power.*

There was something else. The creature could hear the low thrum of machinery and the whine of electricity, even though the soundstage systems had shorted out. Both seemed to be coming from one of the hills in the "outside" area of the set.

The creature made its arms stiff, giving them strength from the shoulders. It drove its hands into the side of the hill with the loudest humming. It was not surprised in the slightest when its hands tore through the façade, revealing the hills to be hollow wood structures. But it did take a moment to appreciate what lay beyond those: the central control room for several soundstages. In the center of the room was a very astonished and suddenly sober Elias Harrysen, the front of whose pants were suddenly wet for reasons unrelated to the soundstage flooding.

Harrysen had watched the thing in front of him on closed-circuit televisions, but going from black and white on a 13-inch monitor to life size – larger than life size, in truth – was a shock. The creature had shed its tar covering in places, and patches of what looked like a red clay structure poked through. Harrysen's mind grasped at what he was seeing, translating it into the only frame of reference he had.

"What the hell are you supposed to be?" Harrysen railed at the creature. "Is this what you animators are doing for special effects? This is my goddamn soundstage, and I *will* destroy it before I let any of you muck it up!"

The special effects man looked around for something that might serve as a weapon. There were few loose items in the room. Most of the equipment was set into large, solid banks. Harrysen flung the one movable object he could lay his hands on – the wheeled office chair he had been sitting on. The creature batted it away nonchalantly.

This one is responsible for what has happened, the creature thought. *He may be fragile like the girl-human. I will stop him, but I must be gentler. Preserve the sanctity of the life spark.*

It was an open-hand slap, but the combination of vegetation, twigs, and cooled tar still made a potent weapon. Harrysen caught one solid blow on the side of his head, which was all that was needed. He slumped, unconscious but alive, against a bank of controls.

As he did, the soundstage wind and rain pitch changed. *These are controlling the storm,* the creature thought. *I must render them inoperative.*

It reached back into the partly collapsed hill structure and wrenched free a steel support beam. With a dozen quick strokes, it stopped the blinking lights on several consoles. As it destroyed the machinery, it could hear the artificial storm abate.

There is aftermath, the creature thought. *I will need to establish communication with the humans, but I do not have the means yet to explain*

79

all this. I have been attacked by a mutant and a human for merely making my presence known. Those in this place are not given to dialog.

The creature became aware that, with the cessation of rushing water, there were new sounds: more were coming.

Leave. Start again.

The creature searched for an exit other than the hole it had made, and found the doorway to the trolley tracks. Through the fake worlds of Elias Harrysen, it made its escape.

CHAPTER SEVEN

Schloss's voice was strong but his eyes were remote.

"Davies burst in on me – us, really, but I'll get to that – while I was in a meeting," the man told. "Actually, I don't know if you can call it a meeting. It was more an intervention. I had been sitting with Romek Perkiel – "

"I *know* Perkiel!" I wouldn't have normally interrupted, but Perkiel's name appeared in the credits of almost every Worldly Pictures set photo in our files. And on those from other studios as well.

"His funeral a couple of years ago was a major Hollywood event," Schloss said. "People know Romek

Perkiel because I wanted them to know Romek Perkiel. I made his career that day."

Schloss had barely taken notice of him previously. Perkiel was blond, surfer-tan, and lanky.

Romek Perkiel had been hanging around the Worldly lot for a few months, taking publicity shots as needed. It was steady work, but it was not what he wanted. Perkiel saw himself as a serious photojournalist.

The assignment editor at the *Los Angeles Times* saw him differently. Give him an assignment, and something usable, although probably not brilliant, would come back.

Worldly sat near one of the more remote La Brea Tar Pits. Perkiel had hoped to cram an assignment for the studio into his day. But for now, he only had one job. Perkiel had been taking photographs of the goo, and cursing his latest assignment from the *Times*.

"Why couldn't I cover the Parade of Roses at Disneyland?" Perkiel muttered to himself as he tried to make tar look interesting. "Or the art display at the Los Angeles County Museum?" he asked nobody, as he tried to capture his own distorted image reflected in a particularly large tar bubble.

"*Shoot the tar pits*, they said," he groused as the bubble burst before he could get his shot. "They'll be great for the paper's 'Preservation of Nature' series."

Perkiel photographed trees and tar. Grass and tar. The sky reflected in tar. Tar on tar. He moved around, trying to find the best vantage for making the pits look as though they were exotic windows into natural history instead of goo.

When a bubble burst and sprayed his vest, he decided he had enough and started to pack his camera.

The soft bubbling behind him suddenly became a much louder sucking sound.

"What the hell...?" Perkiel muttered, cursing the fact that something potentially interesting had started to happen the moment he decided to leave.

He turned, and was face to face with a monster.

"Holy JEEEEZUS!!!" he screamed, as he grabbed at his camera bag, trying to simultaneously back up and aim his camera.

The thing loomed over him, a skeletal frame dripping with tar. Its bright golden eyes fixed on him and it stood, arms down, hands away from its side. A waiting position?

Perkiel was twisting the lens of his camera, sighting in on his target, trying to get the Bog Beast in focus.

And then his camera was gone as the Bog Beast struck upward, gently brushing him back and sending the vintage Bolsey up in an arc before it landed with a soft glop in bubbling tar.

Any rational thought regarding the thing in front of him left Perkiel's mind even as the camera left his hands. Instinct took over. He started running blindly through the woods. His wilderness skills were on par with his photography ability, and he wound up running for 15 minutes in a large circle. When Perkiel finally stopped to catch his breath, he was back where he had started. But at least the creature was gone.

"What *was* that creature?" he moaned. "A Worldly Pictures publicity stunt. Had to be!" But he knew it wasn't. Publicity stunts don't rise out of tar pits without guarantees of being seen. Plus, he would have been tipped off so he could get a photo. Right?

Perkiel needed to tell someone about this. He headed toward the executive offices just beyond the rear gate. There was no guard for some reason and Perkiel entered the first door he saw. It belonged to Irv Schloss, who folks at Worldly said kept the trolleys running on time.

Schloss had returned to his office after what he thought would be the most difficult task of his day – dealing with Elias Harrysen. He was wrong.

Romek Perkiel, his vest still dripping tar, dashed past Schloss's secretary and burst into Schloss's office.

"Monster…did you have a monster out there?"

"Who are you and what are you talking about?" Schloss demanded. "Marion, call security!"

"I just did! Dispatch says they're tied up with some kind of disturbance on the *Tomb of Frankenstein* soundstage, sir. Even Lomax from the back gate."

"What kind of disturbance?"

"A flood."

"Goddamn it. From what, a disaster ride?"

"I don't know. Also, some kind of…monster."

"Wait," Schloss said and regarded Perkiel. "A monster?"

"Monster!" Perkiel blurted. "A Bog Beast!"

Showing his paternal side, Schloss led Perkiel to the couch and wrapped him in a blanket – a blanket that had on many occasions swaddled or provided padding for some of Worldly's finest up-and-coming talent, including Nikie Gordon. If blankets could talk, the stains on this one would have been a chapter guide for many stories.

Right now, though, Schloss wanted Perkiel calm enough to describe what he had seen, or thought he had seen.

"Talk to me, kid," the executive said as they sat on the leather seat.

Perkiel's words tumbled out in a rush.

"A big black thing came out of the tar outside and I was trying to shoot it with my camera but it got away and it's about ten feet tall with huge arms and you gotta do something," was Perkiel's run-on but comprehensive opening statement.

"Now hold on, son," Schloss said. "Tell me about this beast!"

Perkiel paused, took a deep breath, and was off again.

"This tar monster came from the La Brea Pit near east entrance. It chased me! It got my camera!"

Schloss sniffed, cautiously. "You been drinking, son? Maybe weed? Because if you have, I will –"

"No! I swear it! The monster's real, and he –"

"Knocked away your camera, yes," said Schloss. "We'll, uh, get you a new one...if that's really what happened. With a monster."

"It did, I swear it!"

"Right." Schloss went to his minibar and poured a large glass of fragrant gin. "Drink," he commanded, handing it to the boy. "You're in the movies now, so talk to me like your job depends on it – because it does. I want to know everything."

Schloss watched as Perkiel emptied the tumbler in two swallows. Schloss topped it off. He planned to walk the boy past his secretary later, letting her get a good whiff of gin from him.

Still, something *had* happened to the boy, and if it did turn out to be others on the lot screwing around there was either going to be punishment or a promotion, depending on whether or not whatever it was could be monetized.

"All right, again, please," Schloss said softly, trying to sound as concerned for the boy's well-being as he could. "Tell me everything."

Schloss had finally gotten a coherent, if unbelievable, story out of Perkiel when Davies arrived, demanding to speak with Schloss at once.

"There's a flood and some unauthorized makeup creation on my set!" he shouted as he stalked to Schloss's inner office.

"Not. One. Word," Schloss said to Perkiel, as he went to his office door. He stuck his head into the waiting room.

Davies nearly ran into it and knocked over a potted plant as he stopped short. The man was wet, red with rage, and his hairpiece was askew.

"John, give me ten minutes, I'm –"

"Schloss, I don't know what's going on in this studio, but some kind of *creature* just tore apart the set of *Tomb of Frankenstein*!"

"*Bog Beast!*" screeched Perkiel, from inside Schloss's office.

"I thought it was just a leak?" Schloss said.

"A leak? The thing tore the bloody place apart and flooded it. It's utterly ruined. And my Frankenstein Monster was thrown through the air like that crappy mannequin you gave me for the finale!"

This was not stagehands screwing around. This was sabotage – or something. And jobs were going to be on the line. Quite possibly his own.

Harrysen? He prayed not.

Schloss turned to his secretary.

"Miss Crane, get Arbogast at Back Lot Commandos. Tell him I want him here in five minutes to investigate this personally." He turned back to his office, yelling back to Perkiel. "Stay – no, come with me."

Still wrapped in the blanket, Perkiel followed obediently.

CHAPTER EIGHT

Some semblance of normal had returned to Studio 33 by the time Schloss, Davies, and Perkiel arrived. The Bog Beast had managed to destroy whatever controls were releasing the water. Fire engine sirens announced potential help of some sort, but there was no danger of anything burning on what had been the set of *Tomb of Frankenstein*.

Schloss arrived at Studio 33 at the same time Milton Arbogast did. That was fortunate. Schloss had not wanted Perkiel the photographer adding gin-scented hysterics to the mix. Schloss waved Arbogast to his side while Davies scurried ahead to check on his crew – and his movie.

"Milton," Schloss's use of his security man's first name indicated what was being asked was a personal favor. "This is Romek Perkiel. Mr. Perkiel has some very important information he needs to go over with you. Please take him somewhere quiet and give him your full attention. When the set is a little less dangerous, you can do your thing. I will come back for the two of you when I am done."

The security man offered a slight nod and moved the photographer toward the malt shop set.

Inside the studio, Tessa Whiting had kept the handful of crew members on site together in Davies' office. She approached Schloss and briefed him on what had happened.

"The ambulance people already took Nicole Gordon and Andrei Iovan," Tessa said. "Andrei had a sheet over him. Nicole didn't. The crew are very confused, but they aren't hurt. They don't know much. First came the rain, then everything shorted out. Most of them were worried about protecting whatever they were responsible for. Once the lights went out and the floor broke, nobody was paying attention to much other than their own skin. When everything calmed down, they all stood around Nicole, trying to figure out what they could do for her."

Tessa paused, looked around for Davies, who seemed to be in shock. She leaned in to Schloss.

"Most of them are more worried about their jobs."

"Then let's go put their mind at ease," Schloss said.

"There's something else," Tessa pointed at the ruined hill. "After I got everyone together, I went to see what happened with the set there and make sure there were no fires in the master control room. When I got there, I saw Elias Harrysen. I thought he was dead, but when I went to him he shook me off. There wasn't any blood or anything."

"Elias," Schloss sighed. Harrysen's involvement made a lot of pieces fall into place. Monster? Check. Massive set destruction? Check. Hatred for *Tomb of Frankenstein*? Check.

There was only one problem. Harrysen may have been a temperamental artist, but he wasn't a killer. On that, Irv Schloss would have bet his life.

"Where is Elias now?" Schloss asked.

"I had to go back to the rest of the crew," Tessa said. "By the time I could get back to check, he was gone."

Schloss shook his head. "Fine, I'll take care of him. Let's talk to the others first."

They approached the handful of crew and Schloss stood beside Davies.

"Tessa tells me you are all alright, and I am glad to see that," Schloss started. "We do not yet know what happened here. It would be irresponsible of me to guess, but you are in one of the most technologically advanced studios at Worldly, and therefore in the world." He smiled, what he hoped was a rueful smile. "Until we figure this out, we will be closing down this production. But I want to promise all of you that tomorrow you will have jobs. And the next day. You are part of the Worldly family, and we take care of our own.

"We will investigate what has happened here, and we will be making a statement. I know some of you worked with Andrei Iovan before now, and I imagine you are shaken. I am, too. He was a rare talent, and he brought Frankenstein's Monster to life. We will memorialize him, and we will mourn."

The crew members were not mourning. The man was a dick.

"Milton Arbogast will be handling the investigation. I know he will want to speak with each of you so don't leave the lot just yet," Schloss went on. "As you know, Nikie took a few knocks, but from what I understand she will be fine. Thank you for taking care of her.

"While you wait to talk with Mr. Arbogast, I ask each of you able to do so to start detailing what was lost or damaged. Tessa will help organize this.

"If any of you have questions, please contact me directly. Tessa will be able to put you in touch with me.

"One more thing. Elias Harrysen was trying to contain some of the damage from the control room. If any of you see him, you may want to thank him. And if you do, again, inform Tessa. I understand he was hurt in the process, and we want to get him checked out." Schloss smiled. "He's a tough old guy, so don't be surprised if he's having none of it. Just let Tessa know where he is.

Tessa walked Schloss to the door.

"There's one more thing," she said to Schloss. "Nobody is talking about what Mr. Davies said – about a madman attacking Mr. Iovan. For all they seem to know, he fell off his platforms."

"Trying manfully to stay upright in the flood," Schloss said. "Maybe to reach Nicole."

"That's right."

Schloss looked at her. "Thank you, Tessa. I, and the studio, appreciate everything you have done. And we will continue to do so."

Schloss let the vague promise hang in the air as he left.

CHAPTER NINE

If Tessa Whitling was savvy and tactful, Romek Perkiel was the opposite, a beacon of impropriety. The gin and the day's events had caught up with him, and he and Arbogast were seated in a booth far from the malt shop set's counter. Arbogast's arm was around the photographer, as much to restrain him as comfort him.

Schloss arrived as Arbogast was trying to keep the freezing kid warm.

"I've got all the details, Mr. Schloss," Arbogast said quietly. "He's a good kid and calm enough to talk to you, right?" He gave the photographer's shoulder a squeeze.

"Yes, sir."

"Milton."

"Yes Mr. Milton, sir."

Well, Schloss thought, *he's calm if not entirely lucid.*

"I'm going to go talk to the others," Arbogast said, slipping from the stool. "You can tell Mr. Schloss everything you told me."

That meant there was something to tell. That wasn't good, Schloss told himself.

"Mr. Schloss, we gotta go get my camera!"

"Yes…tell me again where your camera is?"

"In the tar pit, and if there's anything usable in it, it's a million-dollar photo!"

Schloss did not bother telling Perkiel that if he had gotten a photo of the creature, his glory would be matched by the problems Schloss would create for him.

"Mr. Schloss, that photo could be my ticket into real photojournalism – not this swamp photography thing."

"We can look together," Schloss promised. "We'll take my El Dorado. You said it's the pit near the east gate? I can get us there quickly."

Schloss covered the kid's head with the blanket and walked him past the ambulances and out through the unguarded gate.

"The sun'll make the tar runny and we don't want that," Schloss fabricated.

They got in the car. Schloss would have normally put the top down, but he wanted as few people as possible to see the two of them together. They spoke as they left the lot.

"Kid, I want to ask you something."

"Sure, Mr. Schloss."

"Exactly how are you going to look for your camera? You planning on sticking your hands in that crap?"

Perkiel looked confused, as if the world had been blurry and was suddenly coming into focus. "A...net? A stick? I could feel around until it bumps into something." He made a vague pumping motion, as if churning dense butter.

"Do you *have* a net?" Schloss asked.

"No."

"A baseball bat?"

"No."

"Well then, we'll have to find a stick. Let's find two sticks, we can use them like chopsticks. You like Chinese food? We'll pick it up like a dumpling."

"Sure, that sounds good. Thank you."

"No problem."

On the off chance that the kid went back to the pit on his own, and the film had survived, Schloss wanted to make sure the camera was never found.

The two parked far enough from the tar pits to gather sticks. Schloss found a solid four-foot branch, easily three fingers wide, that might have come from a fig tree.

By the time they arrived at the tar pit, the kid was subdued; drained was probably closer to it. Plans for his future fame and glory had given way to wondering whether his Bolsey was airtight and if tar could be cleaned off negatives.

"You've got labs that can handle stuff like that, right?" he asked Schloss.

"Tar on film? Sure," Schloss humored him.

105

There were some indistinct tarry footprints near the edge of the pit. Schloss made a mental note to come back and destroy them.

"I think…my camera landed about there," said Perkiel, poking the tar with his stick.

Schloss hefted his stick over his shoulder. He thought about Steve Garvey zeroing in on a fastball. If the kid found something, Schloss would swing at his head.

"I don't feel anything," Perkiel said, leaning further over the sticky surface. He stirred the gunk with his stick.

"Let me help," Schloss said, earnestly but aimlessly prodding the tar.

They fished in the tar for several minutes until the smell started making Schloss dizzy. It was like breathing through your nose over fresh asphalt on a hundred-degree day. "Feel anything?"

"I can't find it," Perkiel wailed. "I can't believe it's gone!" The air seemed to go out of his body.

Schloss put his hands on the younger man's shoulders. He dropped his stick and turned Perkiel to face him. It was time for a moment of truth. Irv Schloss's truth.

"I have known photojournalists," Schloss began. "They have nerves of steel. Go anywhere, stand on anything, push in front of anyone. Keep shooting, no matter what. Some of them have no idea what they've shot until they get into a darkroom. Others just push anywhere without having any idea what they were doing, just trying to line things up in their viewfinder. I've seen them stand on a coffin to get a perfect shot of a widow with one tear running down her face."

Schloss leaned forward, paternally. "You did that, manfully, but the camera is gone. Absent a camera, the world cannot see what you think you saw. A real photojournalist would not have let his camera go.

"I have an idea, one that builds on your strength. Work for us as our exclusive studio photographer. Forget the risks, snap the stars. You will photograph movie action. You will photograph the most gorgeous women in the world. There will be a new camera in it for you, as well. Several, in fact."

Perkiel contemplated the loss of his chance for the gold star, the brass ring…the Pulitzer.

He wept, less than manfully.

"Have you ever wondered, Mr. Leigh, why mediocre artists succeed?" Schloss asked me. "Not the ones whose work lasts forever. I'm talking about the ones who make a day-to-day living when they are alive."

As a writer, I had often fought that same doubt. I answered, "No, Mr. Schloss. Tell me."

"Because they do what mediocre artists throughout time have done when faced with similar situations. Romek Perkiel sold out. He gave up the dream to live in a dream, a dream world others revere. And that is why you know of him."

From a nearby grove, the Bog Beast watched Perkiel and Schloss huddle together before straightening up and leaving. Initially, when they had been prodding at the tar – Bog Beast's entryway to the surface world – the creature had become concerned they were seeking clues regarding its origin.

Now the Bog Beast waited as the sun faded and the air cooled. It had to think, plan better this time.

It wanted to make contact with humans. It *had* to, given events that had occurred in the far deeper and more dangerous world below its own civilization, namely the stirring of the Malignant One and his issue.

The Bog Beast lamented the chaos that its presence had so recently caused, But it had begun to suspect those involved with whatever institution it had investigated were not the types best suited for communication.

The Elders had trained it and sent it to the surface world to study the dominant population – the population whose actions had begun to impact their home, well below the planet's surface. Underground explosions had recently rocked the planet's tectonic plates. Chemicals had seeped into the soil and water. The Bog Beast's people could detect no sign of concern about these happenings from the humans, which they attributed to ignorance. No creatures could do all that knowing they were poisoning others.

Just finding a central communication position had proven difficult. The first structure seemed to be a gathering site, but it was sprawling. When the Bog Beast's people last knew of humans, they had been living in small clusters. They had been much closer to nature, in tune with its rhythms. Now their constructions seemed to be geared toward separating themselves from it.

The Elders would never believe how things have changed since we went underground! the Bog Beast thought.

There was a noise behind it. Arbogast the security man had stepped into the clearing near the tar pool, accompanied by one of his deputies.

"*Holy cripes*!" Arbogast exclaimed. "Look at that thing, will ya?! The photographer wasn't lying!"

"What the hell do we do?" the deputy cried.

Arbogast's answer was already in his hand: he had drawn his Beretta 70, and was aiming at the Bog Beast. "Cut him down! And fast, before he can hurt anyone else!"

"What if it's just some actor, sir?"

"Two bullets, then!"

Arbogast fired, but the bullet must have gone wide – the Bog Beast didn't even flinch.

It had actually been a good shot, entering just below what would have been the Bog Beast's neck. The bullet carried a puff of dirt, tar, and vegetation as it exited just to the right of where a spine might be if the creature had one.

Why do these men accost me? the Bog Beast wondered. *What wrong have I done?*

It did not feel pain, but it could sense the disturbance in its body composition. It could not allow a more powerful version of the human's weapon to be brought to bear against it.

The Bog Beast did not worry about the fragility of the humans. Their weapons had proven them too great a threat. It swung from its shoulders, a two-handed attack that stopped both attackers, knocking them to the earth, where they lay unmoving. As almost an afterthought, it grabbed the weapon the louder attacker had used against it.

This is not something that should be in the hands of excitable humans, it thought to itself.

The Bog Beast turned from the where the two security men had landed. It had a mission, and staying near its entry point to the surface world was not going to further its goals.

Truly this seems a world gone mad! it thought. *I prevent a catastrophe... save lives... and am attacked.*

It began walking from the tar pit, not knowing where it wanted to go, aside from any direction that would not lead back to the studio.

Everything is so spread out up here! it thought.

The Bog Beast soon approached a road. It took some comfort in the similarities between the paved surface and the tar pit. It noted a sign on a post –

Magill's Grain and Feed – and while it could not read the letters, it understood the directional arrow.

That marker...perhaps it will lead me to people! People who won't run away! it thought.

Its shadow, lengthened by the setting sun, stretched down the road ahead of it.

I must seek others! it thought. *Perhaps they will be different... curious instead of aggressive! We shall see!*

CHAPTER TEN

Nikie Gordon did not see Irv Schloss when he walked into her hospital room. Her attention was caught up in a soap opera on the black and white television set, which hung high on the opposite wall.

Schloss had known she was in rough shape, but seeing her was still a shock. She was immobilized by plaster and planks. Her left leg was thickly wrapped, with several chrome pins sticking out of it. Her upper back and shoulders were also wrapped in plaster, although she appeared to have use of both her hands. Her brown, naturally curly hair was matted. Her face – the only part of her body he could see – was badly bruised. Her lips were swollen and split.

"Honey," Schloss said to her, crinkling the paper of a wrapped bouquet of roses.

She winced as she turned her head to look at him. When she spoke, Schloss quietly added the cost of cosmetic dentistry to the studio's liability.

"Irv."

The executive pasted on his sincerity. "Looking good, sweetheart."

"No...gonna be on...c-cover...*Photoplay*... now."

"Don't speak. The doctors say you'll make a full recovery."

"Hunh..." she exhaled with disbelief.

She was right. Schloss had talked to the doctors. He'd had an unethical and very expensive conversation with one.

"Dollface, we will get you the best physical trainers and rehab people we can. This is our gift to you. You're going to be in in the best shape of your life."

"Tennis…out…for…now."

"Only for now. We'll keep you in mind for that big Wimbledon caper movie, *Billie Jean and the King*.

She laughed, and started to cry.

"You should rest," Schloss said. "I just wanted to see you, bring you these," he added as he held up the flowers.

"I-Io…v... van?" she struggled to get the name out.

Fast calculation. Schloss did not want the girl to become hysterical, but he also needed her to think she had only him to rely on through this.

"We lost him, and Davies has gone a little nuts."

Long pause. More tears. Schloss leaned closer.

"Nikie, listen to me. There was a major, a tragic malfunction with the set equipment. I wish we had told you about this beforehand, but this was supposed to be a public relations stunt. A monster attacks the set of *Tomb of Frankenstein*, but the plucky crew carries on. One last gimmick for a movie before the computers take over.

"The only problem was, the elements were out of control. Supposed to be a little thunder and lightning, and then the monster appears. We get a few photographs, and then everything is done. But it all went to hell. Elias Harrysen was trying to fix things, but his control room blew up on him." Schloss had come up with the story on the drive over. He liked how it sounded.

Nikie sighed, a drowsy narcotic sigh. "*Gaslight*, Irv. Not what happened. There was a monster."

The actress was going off script. "Have you told anyone about this, Nikie?"

"Do you think I'm crazy? A beam fell on me. That's all I remember until I woke up here."

Schloss was relieved. "That's good, sweetie. I mean it's *not* good, but it's better that way." He pulled a chair to the side of the bed and sat in it. "Davies is saying the movie set was destroyed by a monster, which is obviously crazy. More than that, if movie sets are destroyed by monsters, that's sabotage. Sabotage is not covered by insurance, at least not at Worldly Pictures. But equipment failure is. Equipment failure means insurance pays off. And people who understand that get their share of that insurance money. Maybe even more than their share. Pays off their medical expenses and lets them live happily ever after."

No word from Nikie, but her eyes were locked on him.

"Anyway, there is no evidence of a monster or a man in a monster suit or a robot in a monster suit. Davies and probably others *think* they saw a monster, but they're wrong. Right?"

"My...head...."

Schloss pursed his lips and nodded. "Of course. It'll feel better and you'll be in front of the cameras again very soon. Those 'monster people' are unstable and will never work in Hollywood again. Crazy talk like that – it gets around. And a person who tells tales out of school doesn't get access to any more tales. The industry protects itself, Nikie. Just like Worldly is going to protect *you*. Nicole Gordon is going to be a star."

"No."

"*No?*"

"No to Nikie Gordon," she said. "Everything hurts. When I'm out of here, I wanna forget about this. New girl. New actress. I don't wanna be the comeback kid."

Schloss was overjoyed, but he wanted to make certain what he was hearing. "You sure? A fresh start would mean a hell of an acting job for you. That's a job for life."

"Long-term contract, Irv. I want my golden ticket."

Schloss knew what he could offer – he had the paperwork with him. "The studio will start you off with three pictures. Promised starring roles. They work, you'll stay above the title. They don't, you'll stay busy anyway. I promise." He produced two copies of a contract from his jacket pocket. "Is that hand of yours healed enough to sign these?"

"Irv, you could chop my arm *off* and I'd be able to sign that contract!"

Schloss fitted his Waterman between her fingers and moved the document around beneath it. With a few loops and whirls, Nikie Gordon was guaranteed lifetime employment.

Schloss tucked both copies back in his jacket. "We'll hire someone to look after you here. I'm going to go get this processed."

He did not tell her that the "someone" worked for Arbogast and would make sure that her mouth said nothing but "ouch" for the next few days.

He poured a glass of water for her, moved the bended straw in her cup so it was closer to her mouth, and after she sipped he put it back on the night table and turned to go.

"Irv," she said through her dampened lips. "Thanks."

"Don't mention it." He smiled. "Don't mention anything."

CHAPTER ELEVEN

"I guess she didn't," Irv Schloss said to me in 2020. "Utter a word about any of this, to anyone. Worldly stayed in business, she made her money, and if this absolves me of any sin I've ever committed, there was nothing in Elias Harrysen's obituary about him committing attempted murder."

"You set the bar high for Hollywood execs who showed empathy."

Schloss looked at me, unsure if I were pulling his leg. I was not, in fact. Before I heard this, that bar was so low an ant would have had to step over it.

"What *did* Harrysen say about what happened?" I asked.

The peaceful look on Schloss's face was replaced by pain. "Not much – not to me, and I guess not to anyone. I had one conversation with him before he moved to Universal – a move I was happy to arrange, thinking, 'Let him destroy *their* sets.' He told me just enough about what had happened to fill in some of the blanks. After that, we were done with each other. He didn't want me near him when he signed his release contract. We handled it through lawyers."

I went over my notes. "There's still one loose end," I said. "What happened to what was left of your security guy, Arbogast?"

More pain in a face already tired of it. "You are going to unearth every skeleton from that period, aren't you? I don't mean literally, right?"

"Well…right. Tell me why people didn't ask about him. Who was he?"

"Easy one. You know Meyer Lansky?"

"The gangster?"

"The same. In 1970 he fled to Israel one step ahead of the IRS. I knew Lansky, and I knew Arbogast, who worked for him. When Arbogast was suddenly cut loose from his Las Vegas employer, I hired him full time."

"Another *beau geste*?" I asked.

"What? The movie?"

"No, I meant – a noble deed. He needed a job, you furnished one."

"Oh. No. I thought I might need muscle around in case anyone yakked out of turn." He shrugged. "You can't put a price on peace of mind."

"Is that all?" I asked. That was a lot to pay for an occasional hall monitor.

127

"Nah, there was more. Union bosses sometimes needed to be more sympathetic to our side of things. Actors occasionally decided they got a bad deal on a movie that made a bundle and wanted to sit out the sequel. You know."

I did. So Milton Arbogast had these skills before he started his four-year stint with Schloss: he had not just worked for Lansky, he had been one of the mobster's top enforcers. He was not just another Hollywood gorilla. Guys like him weren't big family men, either.

"I, uh...I had to get my hands dirty," Schloss confessed.

Again, coming from a Hollywood executive, that was hardly soul-baring. But I knew what he meant. If he wanted to get a good night's sleep ever again, he would have to go to the tar pit and clean up loose ends.

Like bodies.

The story he told me was factual and unromantic, like the man. Schloss said that on the drive over, he realized that day, and maybe every single day for the rest of his life, he would watch for clues to surface…or anything else that might rise from the slow-bubbling tar.

Every. Day. At the pits. Just to eyeball it.

On the drive over, Schloss quizzed himself. What *was* he looking for? Bits of camera? Footprints? Trampled grass? Were the sticks he and Perkiel had poked the tar with still there? Could you get fingerprints from a stick? Should he scatter some used cigarette butts around it?

There *was* physical evidence by the bog: the bodies of Arbogast and his backup.

There were no other markings around the bodies, nothing that indicated they had been found by anyone but him. Carefully, so as not to get tar on his clothes or his hands, Schloss rolled each one into the tar. He did not reveal what he felt about that, though I asked. He just pushed them down with what he thought were the two sticks he and Perkiel had used, and then forced the sticks under the surface as well.

When he was done, Irv Schloss returned to his office at Worldly Pictures. His secretary was long gone, but Schloss wanted to review shooting schedules for the next day. Perhaps there would be some dailies he could sit in on.

Within ten minutes, he was lost in Hollywood magic.

"So that's it?" I asked. "Buy off two witnesses, bury two more, and everyone lives happily ever after?"

"Bury *three*," Schloss said. "You forgot about Iovan."

"Sorry, yes." Unable to be interviewed…out of mind. My bad. "But nobody asked about Arbogast?"

Schloss shrugged. "A man like that has enemies with long memories," he said. "In this case, the enemy of my friend was my friend. People around the studio knew who Arbogast was. That's part of what made him so effective."

"And the other guy?"

"Anonymous muscle, one surely marked for death as soon as he got mixed up in the whole mess." Schloss stirred in his chair, rubbed his belly. "Young man, would you like to get a hamburger? There is a good grill close to here."

He must have noticed my hesitation.

"We can even take your car," Schloss said. "I'm out of the hitting and fixing business."

I did not really think Schloss would try to hurt me. I was his confessor, after all. But that was not the reason. Under normal circumstances I would have loved more time with him. Mob connections…a felon, even if the statute of limitations for destroying murder evidence had run out. Tales from a Hollywood fixer and did he just admit to being a hitman? Jake Vincent would have eaten it all up and gone back for thirds.

But I had my Lynn Brandon story, and it was going to be a good one, even without the Bog Beast. Vincent could have that, and he was welcome to it. If I wanted more of the traditional tabloid filler Schloss

132

offered, I could come back to him later. And at any rate, I do not eat hamburgers.

What I wanted was what Romek Perkiel had turned down in favor of a steady income and the promise of a glamorous career. Unlike Perkiel, I knew how to hold on to a camera. And a tape recorder.

I wanted the Bog Beast. And the Pulitzer that was going to come with it.

I took my leave of Schloss, and I cannot say the old man was entirely disappointed. We had been talking for quite a while, and despite his offer of food the conversation had taken the starch out of him. His head had been dropping for a while, and I suspected his dinner would have to wait until after a nap.

I really did have places to be. Namely, a tar pit just outside the east gate of Worldly Pictures. I did not know what I was going to find there – I had no illusions about finding human remains, or even a submerged camera. I just knew I wanted to go somewhere and organize my thoughts about everything I had learned. It seemed like the best place. And it does not hurt to get the look and smell of a place. Makes for a better article. And longer, if you're paid by the word as I usually am.

I stopped on the way to the tar pits and picked up some cashews and fruit to snack on. I had already planned on obeying all speed limits and traffic laws on the way there – I was carrying the essence of the biggest story I had ever worked on – hell, the biggest story I had been involved in any way on. I was not going to get wobbly because of not eating. Did not trust myself, if I got pulled over by a cop, not to start babbling about ten-foot-tall tar pit denizens.

I did not have to worry. The drive was uneventful, but so was my recon. There were no traces of a couple of 45-year-old scuffles. But it was quiet, and I wanted to soak up the atmosphere, sulfur smell and all. I sat on the sticky ground and studied the tar pit, watching bubbles rise and burst on its surface.

If the talk had knocked the steam out of Irv Schloss, it must have taken a toll on me, too. Dreams, I have heard, are made from day residue and wish fulfillment. Or maybe they *are* part of the collective unconscious, in which case I was collecting.

I probably sound way too cavalier talking about this, unruffled – but I am a journalist first and I have a story to tell, even if it is of my own sudden and inexplicable psychic break. Suddenly, once again, I was seeing through the eyes of a creature I was not even convinced existed.

The still-sane part of me, the journalist, wants to tell the story as it unfolded before – technically, inside – my eyes; more disjointed pieces of the Bog Beast story came to my exhausted brain. In the black mirrored surface of a particularly large tar bubble, I once again saw the world through a set of yellow-gold eyes. Beyond them were images that were not where I was....

Through the Bog Beast's eyes I saw clouds and flashes of lightning. I could feel the thunder, even though there was no rain yet. I had been caught in enough summer storms to know this was going to be a heavy one.

For its part, the Bog Beast appeared to be staying in the shadows, on the sides of a road, avoiding pedestrians and cars.

The cars were – well, let me just say I had not seen a line of cars like that outside of a classic automobile parade. A Dodge Dart, a Chevy Monte Carlo, a Corvette…cars that reflected a nation coming out of a gas crisis in which people still wanted to have fun behind a steering wheel. All looking reasonably new.

Did I say "looking"? Was I looking? Was I hallucinating…*again*?

Did tar fumes release some sort of preserved, prehistoric mushrooms that were altering my reality? Because wherever I was – *whenever* I was – this was not my memory. This was someone – *something* – else's vision, from a time well before an actor named Ronald Reagan had taken the presidential oath of office.

You have read enough, I think, to gather that I am too pragmatic to believe in the supernatural. And in truth, what was happening to me was not the stuff of ghosts and demons, of fairies and leprechauns. We are not talking about vampires here, like that largely debunked Aries VII report from a decade back.

No.

This was the metaphysical, some kind of reality just beyond the manicured fingertips of science.

This was not about bogymen. It was about a *boggyman*.

The Bog Beast, of course, would have no frame of reference for what it was seeing. I suspect that, somehow, terrestrial life forms and basic structures were familiar to it through observation and study. Otherwise, why would it have come here? It might or might not, for example, understand thunder, though I guess that static discharges are present everywhere on – or in – the planet. Falling water was something it would accept readily.

Actually, I did not "guess" as I just said. I felt it. I somehow *knew* it.

I was rapidly becoming less conscious of my own surroundings, and more of – *its*.

I finally surrendered, hoping I would be able to remember at least some of what I would see…

CHAPTER TWELVE

I found myself thinking less with words and more with images as seen through those golden eyes. Fortunately, I still had enough of my own mind overlaid on that of my mental usurper to interpret for myself, and for this report, what I was seeing.

There was a structure, somewhat flimsy – a barn, although it likely was not part of a working farm. What hay was in it was in loose, moldy piles. There were no livestock in it, no vermin about, no pets or fowl.

But there was a hayloft in passably good repair, and a strong ladder that just reached it. The Bog Beast laid the pistol it had taken from Arbogast on one of the hay bales and carefully climbed the ladder. It was going to pause and reflect on its first interactions with humans.

And then, once again, its thoughts covered my own like a mudslide on the Pacific Coast Highway –

I was told my study would be arduous and unending, it thought. *The human animal is a complex thing...a creature long known to be possessed by capacity for exalted good and basest evil.*

It would not have to wait long for more data. Shortly after it had settled in the hayloft, the barn doors opened. A tall, statuesque female-human, with long blonde hair, an off-the-shoulders blue shirt, low-slung green pants, and a scowl entered, followed by a male-human in a yellow shirt, a green vest, brown pants, and a pronounced limp.

Two surface dwellers, the Bog Beast noted. *They also seek shelter from the bursting sounds and driving waters that fall from above! Do none of their species do well in water?*

Their voices rose to the Bog Beast's roost, although it could not understand what they were saying.

"Man, this leg of mine is killing me," the man said. "I never knew a bullet wound could be so painful!"

"Never took one before, college boy?" the woman smirked. "Skipped 'Nam, didja, Ralphie?"

The male-human just grimaced.

"This antiestablishment stuff is *real* political science, not that stuff they laid on you in high school!"

"I need help, Judy," the man said through his pain.

Judy knew that. For all her braggadocio, the Bog Beast could tell she was concerned about the injury. Ralphie had been able to walk on it, but it was still red and pulpy. The bullet Ralphie had taken seemed to have only hit flesh and muscle, though. His thighbones and knee were okay.

She looked around for something to distract both her and him. The Bog Beast watched as her eyes lit on the pistol it had put aside. She seized it, snapped the safety on, and twirled it around her trigger finger.

She plays with it, but does not menace with it, the Bog Beast thought. *Perhaps this one is enlightened in the ways of human tools?*

The female left the male and looked around for something to use as a tourniquet.

"Stinkin' fascist pigs!" she spat. "If they're not ripping off the poor, they're trying to waste them!"

"I told you trying to rob that bank was – "

"Impossible, yeah! So? *So*? We Codys have always taken on big odds, and we need money to do what needs to be done!"

"*Viva la revolution!*" he said weakly.

"Shut it!" she snapped. "If my kid brother wasn't in jail you wouldn't be so flip."

"No. I wouldn't even be here. I did this for you."

"I said shut it," she said, cooling slightly. "I need to get you patched up somehow."

Ralphie obliged and closed his eyes. Normally Judy was sexy when she started on a revolutionary tangent, but the day had caught up with him. They had been on a major adrenaline high earlier and had spent the last few hours running – for him, painfully – on foot. The glorious people's revolution was going to have to wait for morning.

"What this boy needs is some rest," Ralphie announced, laying back on some hay. "All that running... I'm spent! I gotta rest! Rest..."

Judy walked over to him. "Hey, don't fall asleep, Ralphie. It takes dynamite to wake you!" She tried for a joke. "And we used all that up already!"

If he heard, he did not respond. He breathed, heavily but steadily. She crouched by him, examined him, decided he was not pale the way people who were bleeding out were supposed to be. Her relief gave way to frustration, and she suppressed an urge to kick his supine form.

"Nuts, he's asleep already," she muttered to herself. Ralphie was not fat, but he was solid. There was no way she could carry him, and there was little chance of him waking up. Even the thunder was not stirring him. No matter what happened next, he was out cold.

She stood, weighing her options. "If the heat makes this scene now, we're in real trou — WHA?!"

The Bog Beast had observed her ministrations to the man-human, and had begun making its way down the ladder, which creaked under its weight. Judy spun to face it, pointing Arbogast's pistol.

"S-stay away from me!" she screamed.

The female is not as fast to attack as some of the others have been, the Bog Beast noted.

It was wrong. Judy was squeezing the trigger of the Beretta as hard as she could. But the safety was still on. Had it not been, she would have shot the Bog Beast before it reached the bottom rung.

The Bog Beast evaluated her as not being a threat and brushed past her toward the unconscious man. It stooped to him and started tearing his poet's shirt into strips.

The creature's move toward Ralphie cleared her mind. She snapped the safety off and took aim.

It's attacking Ralphie! she thought. *I must stop it! Kill it!*

She stood her ground, perhaps six feet from the Bog Beast, and pulled the trigger four quick times. Three bullets hit. None had any effect, except to wake Ralphie.

"Hey, what's going – HOLY MOTHER!" the young man shrieked, as the Bog Beast leaned toward it, a strip of yellow cloth in its hands.

"It's not possible!" Judy gibbered "Three bullets straight through its head and…nothing happened!"

The Bog Beast ignored them both. It deftly tied the yellow strip just above Ralphie's knee, cutting off the oozing blood flow. It stepped back, observing.

Judy was still frozen, stunned by what she had seen. Ralphie was sitting up, trying to figure out what he was looking at. The Bog Beast evaluated. No apparent threat.

The female showed loyalty to her friend…she misunderstood my actions and attacked!

"This coffin fugitive tied a tourniquet around my leg?" Ralphie asked, breaking the silence.

The Bog Beast stood mute. Judy did not answer. She did not have time to. Four policemen, attracted by her shots, had burst shotguns-first through the barn door.

CHAPTER THIRTEEN

"Police! Drop that weapon, sister!" yelled the first policeman through.

"Everybody against the wall," yelled the second, wanting his own moment. "Move it!"

The two everybodies who were people immediately complied. Judy dropped the Beretta and turned to the wall, meekly placing her palms against its rough planks. Ralphie joined her, hobbling across the floor and grabbing his own section of wall.

The Bog Beast stood off to the side, observing. Its new associates were being threatened, and it needed to assess.

"It's them, all right, sergeant," said the first policeman. "The two who bombed the bank. But who's – good Lord!"

The Bog Beast, shed of its tarry covering, stood before them, oversized, skeletal, muscular, a vaguely humanoid roots-and-red-clay golem.

Four police heads turned to face the Bog Beast. If Judy had not been facing the wall, she almost certainly would have tried something heroic, futile, and suicidal. The policemen's guns had not wavered from the two fugitives.

"What in God's name is it?" breathed the second policeman

Scouts, too? thought the Bog Beast. *They are analyzing the situation. I will wait.*

"Is he human?" one of the policemen asked.

"I can't tell!" said another. "He must have gotten his flesh burned off in the explosion!"

"He wasn't with us!" Judy screamed at them. "Neither were we!" she added when she realized what she had said.

The sergeant had had enough. "You're coming with us. All of you."

Emboldened, another officer grabbed the Bog Beast where its bicep might be. "Whoever – whatever you are, get against the – *aanngg*!"

The Bog Beast had already been grabbed once since it arrived on the surface world. It did not appreciate being grabbed by the male, and it did not appreciate the human's attempted straight arm takedown on him. With a simple arm lift it broke from the policeman's grip – a grip that had helped win arm-wrestling contests both at the precinct and with a local firehouse crew. And then it waited.

Two of the policemen fanned out. "You get behind him!" one said. "I'll try to take him down from the front."

"Be careful,' said the arm wrestler, who was rubbing his wrist with open shock. "He's a lot stronger than he looks!"

This is an attack, the Bog Beast thought. It did not ponder why. Its vegetal structure knotted and reformed within its body into an internal battle formation. It swung its arms, now heavy and hard as any stout tree branch, and the air was filled with cracking sounds as it connected with the two officers advancing on it.

The sergeant was in a position a police sergeant hates to be in – one of losing control. "Look out!" he yelled, filling the air with obviousness. "It's going berserk!"

All was chaos. The fourth policeman was not one for words. He had been cradling a shotgun for more than a day, determined to let it speak for him. And he did, firing three times into the Bog Beast's head.

To no effect.

"Holy cow," the policeman breathed, staring at the barrel of his shotgun in wonder. "I can't put him down!"

The Bog Beast sensed this weapon was more powerful than the others. There would be no holding back, no matter how fragile the human. This human's willingness to use such a weapon unprovoked meant the human was a threat to the Bog Beast's companions.

A single swing of its arm neutralized that threat.

The sergeant saw his men laid out on the barn floor. He had seen the thing take three shotgun blasts to the head without even causing its golden eyes to blink. Nonetheless, the sergeant had been trained to react to such a situation in only one way. He fired his revolver, hitting the Bog Beast, the barn wall, and scattered hay.

The Bog Beast ended that annoyance with a simple, yet highly effective, kick.

There was no motion in the barn. The four policemen were not moving. Judy and Ralphie had not budged from their place against the wall. The Bog Beast watched and waited for a hint about what was supposed to happen next.

Ralphie found his voice and broke the silence.

"I don't believe it!" he said. "No way! I mean, what I've been seein' only happens on T.V.!"

Judy's Marxist training, which consisted of a lot of half-understood books she'd read while high, kicked in.

"That thing is a force that nothing can stop, Ralphie!" she said. "And he's one of us! He's on the side of the Peoples' Revolution!"

Judy dropped to her knees. In thanks, the Bog Beast surmised, since it seemed submissive; but it was actually to retrieve her gun.

As she felt around on the floor, she was inspired. "'To be radical is to grasp things by the root,'" she quoted. "And that thing is *all* roots!"

Ralphie was less convinced. "Maybe…but it could be he's just confused. He only went the violent route when the heat began pawing him."

But Judy was already seeing the creature as a one-man people's army – although she was not sure it was *her* one-man people's army. Ralphie she knew she could keep in check. The creature would only be a useful tool as long as she could control it.

Still, it offered possibilities.

"Let's try to get him to go with us," she said to Ralphie. "Before the fuzz come to again, anyway."

The two began moving toward the barn door. Judy turned to the Bog Beast and crooked a finger.

"C'mon, muscle baby," she said, in a voice she might have used with a reluctant kitten. "C'mon."

Our comradeship is strengthened, the Bog Beast thought. *Perhaps I have finally found friendly surface dwellers who seek to teach me their ways!*

If vegetation had springs, there would have been bounce in its step as it followed.

157

CHAPTER FOURTEEN

The three walked in the woods, avoiding roads and paths. It may have been exhaustion or an adrenaline high but it seemed to Judy that she was lighter and moved faster, as though the soil itself gave each foot a little push as she stepped. She decided the soil must be all rooty. That had to be it. Though, dammit, it really did feel like little palms were lifting her step-by-step.

Given the oddball thing bringing up the rear, that should have been the least surprising thing about the day. If not for the fact that it was as spindle jointed as a skeleton, she would have thought it was some messed-up costume party game or dare.

Initially they heard sirens on all sides, though mostly behind, but eventually they left all the non-forest noise behind. It was all crunch and squoosh as they proceeded.

At Judy's suggestion they waded in and crossed streams whenever they could. Ralphie's leg slowed them, and twice, when the waters reached the wound in his leg, the Bog Beast carried him. Judy marveled at how the Bog Beast's bony limbs went round her companion: one snuggled in the armpits, one round the waist, improbably from the side, not behind.

"Brother's...triple jointed," Ralphie said through his hazy pain.

"Is he hurting you?"

"Nah...it kind of tickles. Like he's made of worms."

159

The Bog Beast had no idea what they were saying, only that the vibrations of their voices were moderate, no longer hostile. It marveled at their contradictions and fragility.

Water gives life, the Bog Beast thought. *Yet I have yet to see a human do well in it. Was it always this way? Did those my ancestors encountered long ago have a greater facility? Is this yet another way they have moved from their roots?*

The vibrations changed the more they made their way through the murky wood. Judy consistently agitated to press on, but Ralphie's leg was hurting more and having none of it. They were resting more and more to rebind his wound and cool it with mud secured by the Bog Beast. Finally, in a thick copse rich with the smell of decay, Ralphie just stopped and dropped.

"Backpack," he said to Judy, wagging a finger at the thinning canvas sack.

She handed it over. Ralphie hacked open a couple of cans with a Swiss Army Knife and he and Judy ate from them. The Bog Beast stood like a golem, still and watchful, unstirred by urgency or the soft wind.

"Give him some," Ralphie said. "He's earned it."

"Eh? Which one?"

"Try peas," Ralphie said. "A peas offering."

Judy made a face.

"Pain brings out the poet in me," he explained.

"We're out of 'em," Judy said and picked up one of the other cans. It might not be a bad idea at that. There was no question the Bog Beast had been useful, both with the cops and with carrying Ralphie, and she

161

still wasn't certain it was controllable. An offering might be smart. She proffered one of the cans toward the mucky statue.

The arrangement of characters on the label meant nothing, though Bog Beast recognized some of them on the side of the can – BLACK ARROW PORK AND BEANS. It had seen them on signs at the Worldly Pictures studio. It had already seen these humans taking the contents into their mouths and guessed their actions were a form of nourishment. This struck the Bog Beast as inefficient: as it walked, its feet absorbed nutrients from the ground. The ground replied to its needs by pushing up. It had pressed against the feet of the humans as well, though they did not accept the offering.

Still, the Bog Beast had been trained as much to be a diplomat as a scout, and that meant accepting whatever well-meaning gifts had been offered. If it hadn't seen both humans eating from other receptacles, it might have suspected they had offered poison. Humans were killers. But it wanted to trust these two. It extended a finger-like appendage, forced it through the metal top, and absorbed a single bean into its body.

Judy and Ralphie watched with amazement; not just the easy penetration of the lid but the almost snake-like swallowing and digestion of the bean.

"*That* is insane," Judy said.

"Efficient," Ralphie said, slightly renewed by the rest and sustenance. "Like bugs...sucking out guts...from other bugs."

The liquid around the bean was sweet – artificially so. The Bog Beast knew of raw cane sugar, but even that was to be used sparingly. This was processed, toxified, and otherwise not healthy for plants and other living things.

There was something else, something foreign. Animal? Was there *animal* in this food? The Bog Beast looked curiously at the two humans, who had scarfed down the contents of the can without hesitation. They did not seem to object to the food, so perhaps the animal presence was something created or modified, like the natural bean surrounded by processed sugar.

Either way, it was not something the Bog Beast wanted more of in its system. It quietly moved the liquefied bean throughout its body. As it did, the Bog Beast uncoiled its finger from the container.

"Just one," Judy observed. "I think our friend was just being polite."

"A good guest," Ralphie said before laying back.

"Yeah," Judy said. "But from where?"

It was dark – even darker than the world below, but without the phosphorescent rocks to provide illumination. There were sufficient breaks in the canopy so that Bog Beast could observe the points of light unseen by its kind for many life cycles. And the larger light, just out of view, which provided a comforting glow. It was smaller and far less stringent than the daytime light. Bog Beast liked it.

That daytime fire – the subterranean had not enjoyed that at all. Not because it dried the body, caking it; not that. It reminded the Bog Beast of the tales told by explorers who had gone the *other* way, below. To the realm of Haydes.

Bog Beast forced itself to think about the Name Most Feared. Here, it was easy to forget. And no one, human or subterranean, dared to do that.

Judy did not appear to be concerned about that dire entity. Bog Beast was glad. A human mind might not be able to contain thoughts so grave....

Judy knew she should sleep. She only hoped she could sleep lightly enough to be at least partially alert. Even without a bullet wound weakening him, Ralphie was going to be dead to the world once he was asleep.

But he was not, yet. Somewhat renewed by the food and relaxation, Ralphie made himself busy, stripping soft green leaves and piling them up. The Bog Beast watched, passively contextualizing and trying to understand Ralphie's actions.

"I've made beds of leaves, brother, dig?" Ralphie said to the Bog Beast. "You…uh…want one?"

The male-human tries constantly to communicate, thought the Bog Beast. *Perhaps in time I shall understand his sounds.*

Suddenly, Ralphie froze. The Bog Beast had scooped a handful of leaves and brought them to a spot below its gleaming eyes. With a subtle crackling, the bunch began to shrink and vanish.

These would be good things to eat, it thought loudly. *Better, at least, than what you had before.*

"He's like a damn guinea pig," the young man said.

"Only bigger and not so pleasingly furry," Judy said.

"*Wheep-wheep*," Ralphie said, thinking earnestly to communicate like the pet he had once had.

Judy shook her head at this dumbshow. "I'm going to gather firewood," she announced, not bothering to wait for acknowledgement. She wanted alone time to sort through her options.

The Bog Beast was disturbed by her apparent leaving. *The female-human was the one who bade me come with them,* it thought. *It will be alone. It may need additional resources.*

The Bog Beast did not so much rise as unspooled upward and started after her, but she whirled on it and put her hands out, palms facing it.

"No, man, I need to be in my own head space, dig? You stay here." She pointed at Ralphie's leaf beds.

The Bog Beast stood, regarding her. She was unsettled. It would do what it did with the young of its kind. After a moment it reached into its chest cavity and pulled out a small lump of lightly colored organic material.

"Gross, man!" Ralphie said. He could not see the action clearly in the dark but he could hear the muddy pulping sound.

But Judy could see. She was afraid to stay – it might be drawing a gun of some kind, made of wood, or maybe a vine slingshot. Or even living guts to eat her. Yet the ground was suddenly adhesive and, besides, she was too transfixed to move.

The Bog Beast reached again, deeper, and withdrew a second, darker lump. It rolled these together just until the colors started to swirl and mix, and then held the ball of its internal material in its hands briefly, letting it firm. The Bog Beast presented the peach-sized ball to Judy.

This will let me at least know of her whereabouts, it thought.

"It's like a big diamond," Ralphie noted. "Or an emerald."

"Or both," Judy said as the colors danced. She extended her palms and accepted it, then looked into the eyes that suddenly appeared no less bright…and calming. As human and Bog Beast connected, soft light radiated outward from the object, touching Ralphie. He seemed confused by the glow as it seemed to seek his leg.

"It's tingling," the wounded man said.

Judy slipped it into her pocket. She could not remember the last time anyone had given her a gift – or cared enough to. Still, she could not afford to be sentimental. Not to Ralphie, and certainly not to the Bog Beast.

"Now you go back and wait," she instructed, adding a shooing gesture. The Bog Beast pivoted and stood guard before Ralphie.

She departed, wondering if this was some kind of trip from which she must soon awaken. Maybe methane in the barn or something.

The ground was less supportive as she moved from the camp. The creature had been great so far, not just thwacking the shotguns from the hands of the fuzz but now. It seemed a gentle being – and obviously protective of them. Of her? Were women revered where it came from, like ant queens? The lack of information and the complexities of the day frustrated her. Ralphie was simple to understand – throw a little revolutionary rhetoric and he became a perfect ally. The new addition to the revolution was something else again. *And maybe, like a Doberman, one that could turn on you suddenly?* she feared.

And there was something else to consider. Ralphie's condition. With no food and no medicine, she could see a no-Ralphie situation in the near future. The teachings of Karl Marx were not going to be much help to him come morning.

Ralphie did not know much about the others with whom Judy shared her anti-Establishment vision. But he knew enough. She did not know if she dared leave him behind.

Judy wandered, forgetting she was supposed to be collecting sticks. She wished she had read fewer radical pamphlets in favor of a book on edible plants or something. Her stomach growled – but then, ahead, there was another noise, too.

Voices! she thought. *Nearby. Damn, damn, damn. Better check it out – might be more fuzz!*

It was decidedly not that. Creeping ahead on tiptoe, pushing branches and hairy vines aside, she peered through an opening and saw trucks, campers, and vans, several of which had *G.A. Wilson's Remarkable Attractions and Funtorium Amusement Rides and Games* painted garishly on their sides.

Judy relaxed. Hope replaced concern. Traveling carnival life was freewheeling...and familial. The only authority was whoever ran the thing. The only law was likely to be a strongman or lion tamer. Coming from the forest, with a living freak show, they might even be welcomed.

They're nothing to worry about, she mused, formulating a course of action as she watched a half-dozen rough-looking young men pass around a bottle that didn't have a label on it. *But hey...I just had a bright idea!*

The revolution, it seemed, had come to the midway.

Ralphie had laughed at the Bog Beast's method of eating.

"I ain't no giraffe, man!" he said, even though he knew the Bog Beast couldn't understand him. "Look," he added, gesturing toward one of the rough rectangles of leaves he had assembled for their companion. "That's *your* sack for the night. Better get some rest while you can!"

Ralphie sank into another pile of leaves, wincing as he shifted his weight on and off his wounded leg.

"I once heard the Indians put mudpacks on injuries," Ralphie said. He chuckled into a surge of pain as he straightened the leg. "I wonder what you would happen if you put your hands on it."

The earthen figure just stood there.

"I guess I'll keep having to wonder," the man said, laughing at the absurdity of the situation – all of it.

The Bog Beast found Ralphie's rich, mellifluous sounds pleasant. It wanted to hear more, and tried to figure out how to inspire those pleasant male-human noises again. It pointed toward its own

175

bed of leaves and Ralphie did, indeed, laugh again, while pointing and then giving a thumbs-up.

"For sleeping, not eating," the man emphasized.

*His words and gestures have meaning, but I cannot comprehend...*thought the Bog Beast. *Wait! He has prepared* three *places. He means for me to rest as he does! The girl-human will take the third place. He is treating me as he does her...and they protect each other. This prone position signifies* acceptance *by the human. I will do as he does.*

Encouraged, the Bog Beast lay down on the foliage bed, curling while it was upright and uncurling to recline. Its action was rewarded by another Ralphie laugh along with a slapping together of his hands. The Bog Beast was pleased, and it allowed its body to go into a dormant state.

Before it allowed its body to settle, the Bog Beast noted that the respiration of the male-human had slowed. He, too, was fast sinking into slumber.

Traveling carnivals meant people, Judy reasoned. People meant hazards or help, depending on the individuals, the group, the circumstances.

Her circumstances were simple. They needed medical attention, shelter – concealment from the law, actually – and they had something to barter for all that. Better to take advantage of what clearly was an opportunity to cut risks and maybe make a few gains.

Judy continued to watch, struck to see how close their own flight had been to a highway, to discovery or freedom. Chance had guided them here.

The carnival was just setting up. There was a faint smell of popcorn, and scent of something other than cold canned goods and rotting leaves had awakened her hunger.

Judy made a wide circle around young men she spotted taking a break. She had a sense of who she needed to speak with, and it wasn't them.

She walked along the games alley, looking for someone she could speak to without being hassled too much. At a ring toss booth, she approached a heavy-lidded skinny teenaged boy who had what looked like daggers drawn on the backs of his hands with a ballpoint pen.

"Hey, young brother, can you tell me where the head honcho is?" Judy asked, putting a little more hip into her movement than she needed.

"Name's George!" the kid responded, flashing a peace sign with one hand and jerking a thumb toward himself with the other.

"You're in charge?"

"Of this booth, yeah."

Idiot, she thought. But she needed allies, not enemies. "Maybe you can show me around later," she said. "For now, I need to talk to the big boss."

His eyes sparked and he pointed to a large Shasta mobile home parked at the end of the alley. She strode toward it as if she belonged.

G.A. Wilson – if that was who answered her knock on the boxy trailer's door – turned out to be a squat cigar-smoking, fedora-wearing man whose rust-colored suit strained to fit over his stomach. He'd been eating a funnel cake, according to the constellation of powdered sugar that dotted his black vest.

179

"You ain't a clown and you ain't an elephant, so you must be – what? A process server," were his first words to her when he opened the door.

"Me? The Establishment?"

He indicated the Beretta that was tucked into her belt.

"Oh, that's part of my scene," Judy said, aware of the way his piggy eyes seemed to be working like little X-ray machines.

"What is your 'scene'?" he asked. "We got a thrill ride called the Zipper. That it?"

If she had known where the fat little ape kept his cashbox, his life might have ended right there. But she kept her cool. "Lemme come in," Judy suggested. "I'm not here for a job, but I've got an act that will pack 'em in."

The owner's expression was dubious but his eyes and lips were eager. It was enough for him to step aside.

The inside of the van was surprisingly organized. A combination of carnival memorabilia and office trappings made her realize that for all his pathetic qualities the little man in front of her was at least something of a businessman.

"So?" the carny boss asked.

"I've got a guy – I don't know if he's a mutant, or if he got burned up, or what," Judy said. "But he's huge, and he's strong, and he's scary. Looks like he's covered in mud."

"The Muck Monster? Not bad. What does he do?"

Judy thought for a moment. She had seen the Bog Beast fight cops and do basic first aid, but didn't think either skill would appeal to the carnival owner. "He doesn't really do stuff, he sort of just is."

"Violent or trainable?"

"Not aggressive unless someone tries to hurt me."

"Beauty and the Muck Monster?"

"Bog Beast," she said.

Wilson liked that and nodded so. "But he's scary," Wilson confirmed. "I can give him some snappy patter – 'Satan's wrath turned me into this,' when we go through Bible country. Plus we could have him do some strong man stuff?"

"Well, he doesn't really talk, either." Judy said. "He's not a guy in a suit. He's the real thing. He's *a* real thing."

Judy thought about showing him the little ball of organic material the Bog Beast had given her. But what would that prove, really? Besides, he would want to use it as a come-on to crowds. It was better kept her secret, something to hock if she needed bread. She felt a twinge of guilt as she thought that; she felt sure it had been given to her with heart, or what passed for a heart.

Or maybe she could sell it to someone else who would appreciate its yin-yang nature.

"All right, assuming I meet this guy and like him, how much were you thinking?" Wilson said, figuring he would shoo the girl from his trailer before going to his safe. There was no way he was going to open it in her presence as long as her hand was near her gun.

Judy had not thought about price. She had no idea how much she could squeeze the boss for, and did not want to let him off the line. "Just lay fifty green ones on me and he's yours." She thought for a moment. "And I want a couple of sandwiches, too. Big ones!"

Wilson was simultaneously relieved and suspicious. A three-headed-chicken in formaldehyde or a cucumber that had a face would normally run him between five and ten times what the girl was asking. He could pay her out of what he had in his pocket. And assuming he did not let her out of his sight until the whatever-it-was had been taken, he had a good chance of getting his money back if she tried to pull a fast one on him. Heck, he might try to take it back anyway.

"Okay, little girl, you've sold me," he said, his pudgy fingers diving into his jacket pocket. He pulled out his wallet and counted out ten five-dollar bills. "Of course, this deal isn't what you'd call legal!"

"Since when has your kind worried about that?" Judy shot back. The big red freak that liked to beat up cops would fit right in. And that reminded her of something else.

"Just make sure you bring at least six strong men, a net, and some heavy chains!" she said.

"Bring? No, sister, you and me are going together. I'll get some of my toughest guys to join us and you can take me to your freak right now."

"All right, but sandwiches first," Judy reminded him. Her mind was already back on the carnival midway, running through the food booths she'd seen. "I want sausage and peppers and meatballs."

"Of course," Wilson agreed, cheerfully.

"Oh, and a first aid kit."

"For?"

"I have a hurt friend. And, I dunno."

"'Dunno' what?"

"Someone might get cut or scraped trying to take the Beast down."

CHAPTER FIFTEEN

After they stopped for her sandwiches, they went to the parking lot on the far side of the carnival.

Judy's instincts about avoiding the six men she had seen when checking out the carnival had been correct. They were not outwardly nasty to her. But their leers and a few not-so-subtle gestures let her know these men were not her revolutionary brothers or anything above sub-human. Bog Beast had more empathy than they possessed among them.

A large part of her hoped the Bog Beast would clock at least a few of them before they brought it under control. Payback for all the years of leering and abuse she had taken.

The group took two trucks. During the ride, Judy began to wonder if these men were up to the task Wilson had set...and what the Bog Beast would do to her for bringing them.

Better play the victim, hedge if I have to, she thought.

The driver followed Judy's directions as they lumped and swerved through the uneven woods. With each jolt Wilson seemed less happy, especially when cigar ash landed in his lap.

At Judy's suggestion, they stopped the trucks far enough from the campsite so that they would not be heard, and walked the rest of the way. When they reached the area where Ralphie and the Bog Beast had bedded down, Judy wondered if it was best to slip in or traipse in. She wondered if the Bog Beast slept. She wondered if he would obey if she motioned him to be still.

She wondered if her head would still be attached to her body five minutes from now. She rested her hand on the gun, uncertain whether it would have any effect.

Wilson was breathing hard as they trudged ahead; then he stopped as if he'd hit a glass door. The creature was everything the girl had promised. Huge, hideous, and just humanoid enough that he could either play it for audience sympathy or pure horror. Either way, he could see his cashbox bulging. *Cashbox*? That thing was going to require him to get a second safe, at least. Or possibly a second show just devoted to the Bog Beast. He could leave that turkey George in charge of the two-bit carny and go out on the road with it, like P.T. Barnum and the Cardiff Giant. Although this giant, the girl had told him, could move.

As Wilson was mentally earning and spending thousands of dollars, one of the men nudged another and gestured toward the sleeping Ralphie. Judy overheard a soft comment. "Is that something too?"

Wilson glared at them, and pointed at the larger supine figure. He silently raised three fingers, curled his ring finger, curled his middle finger, and pointed again with his index finger.

The six men looked at each other. No one moved.

Judy smothered a laugh. "Your toughest guys," she tittered.

"*Net*," Wilson hissed.

One of the lugs produced a large circular net from the back of the truck. Wilson stood back as the men spread it and tossed on a count of three. By a count of four, the Bog Beast was on its feet. With a guttural "Aanng!" – the first noise Judy had heard it make – the tendrilly titan lashed out with its right arm and rendered the flimsy thing useless. In the same swipe it knocked two of the roustabouts senseless.

"He's breaking through the net!" Wilson yelled unnecessarily. "Get the chains!"

The underground dweller fought savagely as heavy towing chains wound around its shoulders and torso. It rolled its shoulders, sending waves of chain that wrenched free of its would-be captors' hands. Its earth-claw appendages raked in wide circles around it, hitting and occasionally tearing flesh. As the chains circled it, it spun, trying to free itself before it could be fully shackled.

It glimpsed Judy hanging back from the melee, watching. It paused, uncomprehendingly.

Is she caught too?

The Bog Beast glanced over at Ralphie, making sure he was not endangered. Ralphie was still asleep. That was enough opportunity for one of the braver men to loop a chain around the Bog Beast's ankles and topple it.

"Whew, we got him!" another man, who had not yet realized his cheek was flapping bloodily against the side of his face, said.

"Start dragging him toward the trucks!" Wilson yelled, trying to establish that he had somehow contributed to the group's efforts. "Hurry!"

The Bog Beast realized the chains were too strong. It had no leverage for countermeasures. As it was being dragged, it analyzed its situation. The seven human men had not used the dangerous projectile weapons that others had, which meant they did not intend lethal harm. But they nonetheless had subdued the Bog Beast.

It wondered whether it had done something wrong, perhaps presenting itself as a threat. It reviewed its actions. Should it have eaten more of the offered nourishment? Had the girl somehow sensed the weapon she now wore was something it had briefly carried, and that made it a threat?

The Bog Beast turned its head toward her, and its golden eyes saw her standing, arms crossed in front of her, watching as it was dragged away.

Its eyes also saw two of the attackers sprawled on the ground, their life essence and internal workings spilling on the ground, nourishing the earth. The Bog

Beast was saddened they had been recycled by its hand, but they had not furnished an option.

It had expended much strength fighting them. It would rest now and see where they went.

The Bog Beast had come to the surface to learn and explore, to prepare for events the Elders feared were to come. It had given Judy a Healer, connected to the earth – and while she saw it help Ralphie, she had not tried to aid the others.

As the surviving men gruntingly raised the Bog beast into the second truck, it wondered if there was any hope for the plan the Elders hoped to enact....

CHAPTER SIXTEEN

Man, that was the Third World War, Judy thought as the trucks drove off. She looked over at Ralphie on his arboreal bed. *And dig old VIP over there. He slept through it all.*

What a lump. What a disappointment.

Maybe it was time to go solo. She did not even feel regret at that thought. The Revolution was more important than any one person...and Ralphie, poor Ralphie, was barely even that.

There were already too many people associating her and Ralphie with the big red freak. There were probably cops looking for whoever had bombed the bank and beaten up their buddies. And the carnival people were weird and unsettling. Besides, when Wilson started to advertise the Bog Beast, where would John Law go directly?

It was *definitely* time to go.

She looked over at Ralphie.

She grabbed his ear. Twisted, letting her fear get the better of her. Ralphie blinked awake and gave her a loopy, yawning grin.

"Morning already, Judy?"

"No, dummy, we –"

But Ralphie had already struggled to his feet.

"Hey," he said, putting his weight on his injured leg. "My leg feels okay! I gotta tell that brother he's got the magic tou—"

"Forget it," Judy cut him off, curtly. "Your boyfriend's gone!"

"Gone?" He looked over at the bed of leaves. It looked like a tornado had struck. "What happened?"

"There's a carnival close to here," Judy said. "He's in a cage by now." She fanned the wad of bills Wilson had given her. "I sold him, dig? Soldiers in the People's Army have to eat, y'know!"

She waved the grease-soaked paper bag containing the two sandwiches at Ralphie. "I got breakfast, too, so let's eat up and move!"

Ralphie was not interested in sandwiches. He grasped for an insult. "Judy, you smell!" It was not as strong as he might have hoped, but he had never been good with words. "Do you know that? You... *smell*!"

The outburst took Judy by surprise. She took a step back from him.

"Huh? What're you getting uptight for?" she asked, suddenly aware of exactly how large a man Ralphie was. "He wasn't human!"

"We're going to get him back, Judy!" Ralphie stood, gesturing with one finger in the air, the way he had seen Judy do when she was lecturing on the evils of the system. "Even if he wasn't the equal of us great… great…homo sapiens!"

Judy stood her ground. "Hey, I'm the leader here, remember? We've got more important things to do!" It was time to teach the ape a lesson about authority and control. "You want the freak back, go get him yourself. That way!" She pointed in the general direction of the carnival, expecting the prospect of following nebulous directions would confuse Ralphie into obedience.

But Ralphie saw marks and tracks of where the Bog Beast had fought and been dragged. He imagined his "brother" being bound and gagged – the Bog Beast's lack of an apparent mouth didn't enter into his thinking – and dragged away to enslavement. Something within him snapped.

"Right on, baby, I'm going!" Ralphie said, turning from Judy. "And I'm not coming back!"

That did not work for Judy. If the revolutionary cell was going to splinter, she would be the one doing the splintering. This was not in the plan. This was not in the plan at all.

Reason, Karl Marx once said, has always existed, but not in a reasonable form. Judy did not know that quote, but it would not have mattered. She was well beyond reason as she drew the Beretta from her belt and aimed it at Ralphie's back.

"I guess you forgot the rules!" she yelled at her soon-to-be-former. "Forgot that the price for running out on this outfit…is death!"

She pulled the trigger twice, hitting him just below his left shoulder blade.

Ralphie spun, fell against a tree, which he grabbed for support.

"Y-you shot me… in the back! You, w-who call the establishment all murderers…" he gasped.

A thin line of drool leaked from Judy's mouth. Her eyes were unfocused. "You talk too much, baby," she said. She sighted along the gun barrel, aiming at Ralphie's chest. "So long. It's been swell!"

Click. Click.

"I'm out of ammunition. I don't believe this!" Judy said to the woods.

Ralphie was moving. *How many bullets was it going to take to put him down?* She wondered. Clearly at least one more than she had.

He stooped, scrabbled among the roots of the tree he had braced himself against. Judy turned from him and started to run.

The rock he threw at her was the size of a baseball, and it had a pretty good amount of thrust behind it. It caught her just behind her left ear, and it was jarring. The big lummox *had* been strong.

He was not going to get another shot at her. She sprinted from the clearing and ran, not knowing where she was going except that it was away from the carnival – and from Ralphie, who with the effort of his throw had sunk to his knees and was wheezing. Her head hurt, and with every step she thought she was going to throw up, but on she ran.

CHAPTER SEVENTEEN

Ralphie had struggled to his feet, but it was not easy. He was once again gripping the tree, but he knew that simply standing, holding it as he bled out, would be the last thing he did.

The truth was whatever he did next was probably going to be the last thing he did. Ralphie was enough of a warrior to know when a wound was fatal. He was also enough of a man to have a sense of duty for his fellow revolutionaries – even if a particular revolutionary was made out of earth and wood and vines.

That sick chick, Ralphie thought. *I don't have time to go after her and knock some sense into her dumb head.*

That did not leave him with many options for making an impact on the world. But it did leave him with one.

Gotta get that brother out, he thought. *Everybody's gotta have freedom.*

He had a vague sense of where the carnival was, based on the direction the men had taken the Bog Beast. And what the hell, if he had to die, a corpse would be one more far-out attraction on carnival grounds.

Walking was painful, but Ralphie was determined. Despite what Judy had thought, Ralphie had enough smarts to follow car tracks. He looked carefully at the zigzag treads the carnival workers' trucks had left in the earth, and started in their general direction.

The Bog Beast had been laid into the bed of a pickup. It had a moment of confusion when the truck started and began to move forward.

Alive? it thought. *Do I feel breathing under me? Is this some sort of transport beast?*

The pickup was a Chevrolet Longhorn, but the irony would have been lost on the Bog Beast, even if it had known the model. At any rate, it quickly dismissed the notion of life: the Bog Beast felt no sense of anything organic under it.

There was swearing from the carnival men, perhaps rage at the loss of their comrades. The Bog Beast did not like these sounds. They were not like

Ralphie's laughter. People made complex noises. Even if the Bog Beast had not been wrapped in chains by the men, it would have been hesitant to attempt to communicate with them. Instead, it waited.

The ride did not take long. The trucks headed back toward the small workers' encampment on the edge of the carnival where Judy had first seen the workers. The Bog Beast heard the short, fat, rust-colored human say something, but could not make out what he was saying. All it knew was that it was lifted from the truck bed and – with more of that unpleasant laughter from the carnival men – carried.

There were several large structures, and the men bore the Bog Beast toward one of them. One ran ahead and opened a door, revealing a dark interior. At this, the Bog Beast began to thrash. It could not see what waited for it inside the structure, but it was not happy about finding out while being wrapped in chains.

It did not have much choice. It struggled and thrashed, and managed to leave a solid tar-and-red-clay mark on the metal door frame of its would-be prison, but the men holding it had leverage. With a shout, they unceremoniously tossed it into the dark and shut the door. Clanking noises followed.

The dark itself was not a problem. The Bog Beast's race was used to low light. The immobility was annoying, however. That was a new sensation and the subterranean did not enjoy it.

The carnival men had tied the Bog Beast up as if it were a human, and therefore subject to the movement limitations of a human body. It was not, of course, and it relaxed, focused inward, and began shifting its internal structure. Within a few minutes it had managed to free an arm. From there, it shrugged off the rest of the chains easily.

The Bog Beast stood and pushed against the walls of its prison. *Flimsy,* it thought. *With enough force, I might be able to go through these. But...what is on the other side? All who took me were man-humans. They might have the large versions of the weapons that do so much damage.*

Better to wait and see what is to come, it thought. *If I must use force, I will do so based on my opponents' attacks. I will let them make the first moves.*

The Bog Beast had no way of knowing, but guards would not have been a problem. One of the men needed to be taken to the carnival infirmary, and another was drafted to escort him. The rest were under strict orders from Mr. G.A. Wilson to absolutely, under no circumstances, leave the Bog Beast's trailer unguarded.

Which meant that, as soon as Mr. G.A. Wilson had left their encampment, the would-be guards piled into a truck and headed toward a roadhouse, their pockets stuffed with Mr. G.A. Wilson's cash. Their prisoner, they had to have reasoned, was trussed with chains. It wasn't going anywhere.

The Bog Beast used its incarceration to review its actions. *Have I done anything which would cause me to be viewed as a threat? I cannot think of a serious offense against the man-human or the girl-human I traveled with. I was treated as one of them.*

It tried another tack. *Perhaps one, or even both, of the humans I was with did* not *have my well-being as a priority, despite the way I interpreted their actions.*

And there, confusion yielded knowledge as the Elders said it must:

I will need to be even more cautious regarding my prolonged exposure to any given humans. I clearly do not understand them yet!

There was a noise at the door. A scratch. A jangle. A thud.

The door opened, and Ralphie stood, weaving, in the frame.

"C'mon, pal," he wheezed. "I picked the lock. You're a f-free bird again." Ralphie swung himself to the side, showing the Bog Beast that it could leave, but the effort was too much. Ralphie collapsed, the last of his strength leaking out of the two holes in his back.

The Bog Beast took a few tentative steps from the trailer in which it had been imprisoned. It turned to

Ralphie, looking for guidance. It saw pain. Where was Judy? Where was the Healer?

From his kneeling position, Ralphie turned his head and looked at the Bog Beast. "No...d-don't wait for me, y-you dummy..." he gasped "Get out of here b-before they..."

That was all Ralphie had strength for. He pitched, face first, onto the ground.

The Bog Beast was not used to rushes of conflicting input. Among its own people, motives were usually directly expressed through actions. It had viewed the man-human and the female-human as a single unit with an identical mindset. But based on the last of each of their interactions it had observed, they appeared to operate independently.

It knelt and examined Ralphie. Despite its limited understanding of human physiology, it quickly reached a conclusion.

He is without life! The Bog Beast realized. *That causes me great sorrow...and anger. I suspect the female human was responsible for my incarceration...and she could then be responsible for the noble one's fatal wounds!*

It had another unsettling thought. It had left the weapon where the female human had first found it. Was *it* responsible for the man-human's spark being extinguished?

I need information, it thought. *I will go back to the female-human and attempt to communicate, not as a friend, but as a scientist. Perhaps there is an explanation for this.*

There might well be such – but the Bog Beast did not think it would be satisfying. Ralphie's wounds were inflicted with the same kind of weapon the other ones had utilized back at the barn.

It began walking in the direction of the camp.

Judy would have sworn she had been running for hours. She had not. The rock Ralphie had hit her with had raised a good-sized egg on the back of her head. It also blurred her sense of time, direction, and balance, as well as her general sense of being – she could not tell whether she was hungry or nauseous.

She stopped running and took stock of her situation. She had dropped the gun at the campsite – and damn, damn, damn, would she have to go back and get it? Or was it best to keep moving? But the hunger-and-nausea question was easy to sort out. Return for the gun, no. Go back for the sandwiches – yes.

Her vision blurry, legs wobbly, she nonetheless retraced her steps. Somewhere along the way she lost the thing the Bog Beast had given her. She would look for it later.

Reaching the camp, she saw at once that Ralphie was gone. Found by someone? Or did he crawl off to die? *Was* he dead? Would he rat on her? To have a murder rap on top of everything –

No time to consider that now. Her head hurt worse than ever, her stomach slightly less. She sought and found the meatball and sausage heroes. They were cold and congealed. This did not stop Judy as she ripped open the paper sack and took wolf-sized bites.

That cheap bastard Wilson had not given her a lot of sauce, and the sandwiches were dry. Still, she tore off great unchewed bites, eagerly anticipating finally having something in her stomach. If only her forehead and temples did not throb, she might enjoy –

She vomited the first torn pieces that entered her stomach. Choked. Light flashed behind her eyes.

Damn, thought Judy, although no sound escaped from her. She moved to a tree and slammed her back against it, which only made the pain worse. She fought to stay upright. She began to sweat. *Goddamn goddamn,* she thought, as she saw brown fog creep into the corners of her eyes. The world turned round and round.

Judy tumbled to her knees, clawing at her temples, pounding on her chest. Her last thought before everything went dark was the ultimate revolutionary thought:

The Man won.

She tried once more to rise and then gave up, piling on indignity as her head struck the same rock that had been thrown at her.

The Bog Beast found Judy sprawled on the forest floor. It knelt beside her inert form.

She too is without life, it thought. *But I do not see any of the red fluid I saw in Ralphie or other instances of humans without life. It is evident her head struck this rock as she fell – a strange accident.*

The Bog Beast departed in the direction that still held her footprints. Along the way it found the small Healer it had given her. It cupped the ball in its hand and absorbed it. When it was finished, the Bog Beast continued its journey.

The same unknown forces of fate are at work here as well as where my people dwell, it thought. *My knowledge increases with each experience on the surface. I wonder what next lies ahead for me?*

CHAPTER EIGHTEEN

I was wondering that myself.

When we wake from dreams, there is a moment of disorientation – not the sitting-up-in-bed-gasping way too many movie directors like to show, but a blinking sensation of "*I was there, and now I am...where?*"

Eastern philosophers also believe that in that moment is pure truth, before our minds return to their bias of differentiation and judgment.

I did not have any of that enlightenment, because I did not feel as though I had just woken up. It was more like having a virtual reality headset lifted off me. For the entire time I had been wearing it, the saga of the Bog Beast had been my reality. Now, VR helmet off, this was my reality.

Except there had been no helmet. There had only been a pair of yellow-gold eyes, and I had seen through them. Most of the time, at least.

I did not really care about the two hippies. They were bit players, and neither Jake Vincent nor anybody else was going to pay for their story. On the other hand, the story of the Bog Beast....

I had a lot more information than I did before I sat down at the side of the tar pit. But as with the best of these stories, more information only led to more questions. I couldn't try to follow the path the Bog Beast had taken after it left the girl: forty-six years on, that trail was cold. I could, I suppose, try to track down the carnival people, but I had only the vaguest sense of who or where they had been. I could go through some newspaper morgues looking for advertisements, but I did not have high hopes for finding anything. Nearly five decades on, they might not be alive, any of them.

But I did have a path to follow, and it was right in front of me, albeit straight down.

If I wanted to know more about the Bog Beast I was going to have to go into the tar. And beyond the tar, to see whether I could follow its trail.

That might sound crazy – it *was* crazy – yet in the space of two days I had uncovered a conspiracy to hide a studio disaster, give an actress a completely new identity, hide the evidence of two killings…and been presented with both second- and firsthand evidence of some sort of organic bog monster. I cannot be faulted for not thinking straight.

But that did not mean I was thinking like a lunatic.

A few years ago, I did a feature on Navy SEAL stunt extras. Made friends with a couple of them. One, Chris Olson, actually took the time to tutor me in diving skills – the kind you are not going to be taught when prepping for a leisure dive in Aruba.

I had written an article that made the SEALs look good. The Navy had loved it and Olson had been rewarded for his role. Which meant he owed me a favor.

"You want to *what*?" was his reaction when I told him my plan, and what I hoped he could equip me for.

"It would be a blind dive," I said. "Lots of visually impaired people go scuba diving."

"And lots of visually impaired people do not," he responded. "Why do you have to go into a *tar pit*?"

"Because it's there?"

Olson scowled so hard I thought FaceTime would break. "Seriously. Why?"

"I have geological soundings that show there is water beneath the tar," I cheerfully lied. "And in that water are preserved skeletons that will blow people's minds. Get me through the tar and I'll never have to write about who wore what on the red carpet during Oscar night again. That's why."

"What's wrong with looking at pretty women on the red carpet?"

"Get me into the tar and I'll give you my credentials the next time I'm supposed to cover one,"

I said. At least that was not a lie – assuming I came back.

Less than 24 hours later, after sending the Nikie Gordon article to Jake Vincent – to what was, for my editor, enthusiastic praise – I was in possession of some of the most sophisticated diving equipment I had ever seen and never used.

This was real. It was going to happen. I was either out of my skull or headed to the greatest scoop since the *Belfast News Letter* debuted the Declaration of Independence. Vincent would receive a delayed-delivery email declaring my intentions.

I carried my gear to the remotest of the La Brea pits, at night, having planned my entrance carefully during daylight. I donned the suit, grunting and huffing, then stood on sturdy flippers at the edge of the pit.

A pit that had eaten mastodons and saber-toothed tigers with ease. I was going in armed not with tusks or fangs or claws but with an old school notepad and two pens tucked in a sealed pocket. Evolution had given me writing but clearly not a sharper mind than a denizen of the Pleistocene.

I switched on the breathing apparatus and heard my own life in my ears. The clock was ticking, the gauge numbers moving, so there was no time to waste.

I wasted some anyway. I tried to invoke the Bog Beast, to re-establish a connection. I looked into the tar, concentrated on a large bubble to empty my head, but did not succeed. My surroundings were still my surroundings.

Or *were* they? The bubble suddenly seemed to invert, as if it had been sucked back into the tar. Then I wondered – am I looking up into it?

I suddenly found my legs moving and my feet in the tar and then I did not have to do anything more as I sank into the gooey substance feeling the pressure on my abdomen increase, and then my chest, and finally on my head…

COMING SOON!

Wrecage

About the Author

Richard H. Levey is a seasoned investigative reporter whose beats have included the business, political, and nonprofit sectors. His sardonic "Loose Cannon" business commentary column was a must-read for the better part of a decade. Richard's magazine work includes articles on UFOs, airplane disasters, conspiracy theories, sensational crimes, rock and roll, and healthy living. He has also ghostwritten bestselling books of political commentary and true crime. *Digging Dirt: Seeking the Bog Beast* is the result of his lifelong devotion to comic books – and Atlas Originals in particular. He lives in New York City.

Made in the USA
Middletown, DE
11 August 2020